—Tea &—
SYMPATHY

A Tea & Sympathy Mystery

BOOK 1

J. NEW

Tea & Sympathy
A Tea & Sympathy Mystery
Book 1

Copyright © J. New 2021

Cover design: J. New.
Interior formatting: Alt 19 Creative

OTHER BOOKS BY J. NEW

Chapter One

"**G**OOD MORNING, LILLY. A fine morning." The jogger said as he approached the cyclist.

"Morning, Peter. Isn't it lovely to have the first signs of Spring showing through?" She replied, coming to a stop and causing the grey cat, dozing in his carrier in the front basket, to meow plaintively. "How's Charlotte doing, by the way?"

"Brilliantly, and it's all down to you. I can't thank you enough for your advice. Things are much more peaceful in the house now. Although the music is still louder than I'd like."

Lilly laughed. "That's teens for you, Peter. But I'm glad I could help."

"Well, I for one am relieved you're still on hand to dispense excellent advice, even though you're not with the paper anymore. How's the new shop going?"

"Extremely well, as a matter of fact. Which is an enormous weight off my mind as I sunk almost everything I had into it."

"Excellent news. Long may it continue. And I'm sure it will, considering this country practically runs on tea. And talking of running, I must get on. I'm trying to beat my best time." He said, tapping the Fitbit tracker on his wrist.

"Of course. Actually, while I remember, could you let your wife know the Alice in Wonderland tea set she ordered has arrived?"

"Will do. Thanks, Lilly." He started his stopwatch and set off running again with a last wave over his shoulder.

Lilly Tweed, former agony aunt with the local newspaper now a purveyor of fine teas and owner of The Tea Emporium in the centre of Plumpton Mallet, gripped the bike's handlebars and once again set off down the riverside path on her way to work. Pedalling through the tunnel which passed under one of the major roads from town, she entered the park and took a deep breath. After the dark, cold and wet days of winter, it was a joy to cycle to work again. To see the small buds appearing on the trees and the shoots of daffodils valiantly pushing up through the grass.

She sped along the path, the wheels kicking up the last of the fallen autumn leaves, and turned left up the steep hill at the edge of the park which led to the town. From there, it was a brief journey to the market square and her shop.

Plumpton Mallet was a historic market town with the cobbled square being its oldest part. A firm favourite with tourists who came in their droves to walk through the woodland, picnic on the little stone beaches beside the river, then finish with a meander around the shops and cafes in the square itself.

The Tea Emporium was housed in the old apothecary shop, and although it had had several retailers since then, the interior had remained authentic, with floor to ceiling shelves, and cabinets with row upon row of miniature drawers with dainty brass handles. It was the perfect set up to house Lilly's merchandise and display the range of quirky china she sold.

The exterior was double fronted with large bay windows flanking a recently painted cream door. The door furniture was also brass, including a knocker in the shape of a teapot which Lilly had found at an antique fair years ago and bought on a whim.

She dismounted, leaning her bike against the window and retrieving Earl unlocked the door and entered.

*I*NSIDE, LILLY RELOCKED the door and let Earl out of his carrier. He sauntered across the wooden floor, stretching each individual leg in turn, then jumped up to his favourite spot, the window. Delicately avoiding the items on display, he walked on silent paws to his bed and curled up. It was an odd place for him to choose, but it was the position he obviously felt safest and happiest, and there was no doubt about it: having a cat in the window certainly made people stop and look. Earl Grey was good for business.

He'd turned up barely a week after she'd opened, a thin, filthy and flea ridden bag of bones with a scar on his nose and a chunk of his right ear missing. Lilly hadn't a clue how he'd ended up on the streets, but he wasn't doing well. She'd promptly taken him to the local vet for a check-up and adopted him immediately. It had been touch and go for a while, but Lilly had poured all her energy into saving him. That, along with his fighting spirit, had seen Earl over the worst and well on the way to recovery. Now he was as much part of the shop as she was, and her first order of the day had been to install a cat flap in the storeroom door at the rear of the shop. There he had access to food and water as well as a litter tray and another bed. But he still preferred the window.

Lilly repositioned the *Help Wanted* sign in the other window, then began getting ready for the day ahead. The Tea Emporium had only been open for just over two months, but word had spread quickly thanks to some free advertising for its former employee in the Plumpton Mallet Gazette. Now though, it was necessary to take on her first member of staff.

After she'd gathered the post, the morning newspaper and set up the rest of the shop, she turned to the last job, decorating her bike. On the pavement outside she chained the bike to an old post and hung the open sign on the handle bars. She filled the basket with colourful pots packed with spring flowers and fixed another flower basket on the seat. Her last job was to put up the *Tea of the Week* sign. She'd chosen Echinacea because of its benefit to improving cold, flu, and sinusitis symptoms. Perfect for the time of year. That done, she went back inside and brewed herself a cup of Ginkgo Biloba, known for improving both brain function and vision, and perused the paper while waiting for her first customer of the day.

The front-page story was a rehash of one that had run previously, with very little in the way of updates. There had been a break-in at the local university and various small, but high cost pieces of equipment and a number of pharmaceuticals had been stolen from the labs. So far the culprits hadn't been found even though there were continuous interviews being carried out with students and teachers alike. Popular opinion was the drugs were being sold to addicts somewhere out of town. Lilly could almost hear the tone of derision in the piece at the failings of the police to solve the thefts. The author wouldn't be doing themselves any favours by making an enemy of the local police officers. She glanced at the byline and noticed Abigail Douglas had written it; the new agony aunt. Lilly had heard rumours that the column wasn't doing well, was Abigail trying to set herself up as an investigative reporter instead?

When the small local paper had been taken over by a much larger concern, they had offered Lilly redundancy. The new owners already had an agony aunt who apparently intended to move to Plumpton Mallet, and Lilly suddenly found herself middle-aged and unemployed. It was a terrifying prospect but was just the push she needed to try to make a go of a long-held dream; to open her own tea shop. If she didn't grab the opportunity now, then she knew she never would. A combination of her redundancy money, the majority of her savings and a small loan from the bank and she had secured the premises. Two months later, it looked as though it was paying off. There wasn't a day when she wasn't busy.

She turned to the page where the agony aunt column usually was to find it absent. Lilly had worked hard on her column and through good advice, a genuine desire to help and her interest in people, she had turned what was to all intents and purposes a 'filler' into an integral part of not just the paper but the community. She sighed, it saddened her to find it was no longer popular, but it wasn't her concern now she had her own business to look after.

She was just disposing of the paper when the shop bell tinkled. Time to get to work.

ER FIRST CUSTOMER entered and announced themselves with an almighty sneeze.

"Kate, you poor thing."

"Sorry, Lilly. Can you help? I'm getting nowhere with my cold medicine, I think I've become immune to it, and I want to see if something more natural will work."

"Of course, have a seat and I'll put the kettle on."

Kate took one of the bar style stools at the counter while Lilly selected several samples.

"Is it a cold or more sinus symptoms you have?" Lilly asked, putting a teacup and saucer in front of Kate.

"Sinus problems, although I'm just getting over a nasty cold as well."

"Do you have a sore throat at all?"

"A little, although not as bad as it was."

"Well, both Mint and Echinacea will help with the sinus problem. As will Ginger, and it also helps relieve congestion. If you have an infection, then Thyme will help. I've also just got some Japanese Kuzu tea, which helps with cold and sore throats."

"So many to choose from. What do you suggest?"

"I'll brew you a cup of Echinacea, I think that's the best for the sinus problem and as **Tea of the Week** it's on special offer. Have you eaten, Kate?"

"Yes, I had porridge for breakfast."

"Good. You mustn't have this tea on an empty stomach. You can have a cup two or three times a day until you feel better, but don't take it for more than ten days. Also ginger will help fight any infection and reduce inflammation, so you could take some for later if you want?"

Lilly let the tea steep in the small teapot for three minutes, then using a decorative strainer, poured a cup for Kate. She took a deep appreciative breath and smiled.

"It smells lovely. Hope it tastes as good."

She took a sip and nodded. Within five minutes she'd finished the cup.

"I feel better already. I'll take it and some of the ginger as well. Thanks, Lilly."

With her purchases wrapped, Kate asked Lilly if she mended tea sets?

"It's the handle of one of the cups which has come off. I'd like it mended as it belonged to my mum."

"I'll need to see it before I can tell you if it's possible. Can you drop it in some time when you're passing?"

"Yes, I'll do that. Thanks, Lilly. See you soon."

After Kate had left, there was a steady stream of customers. It actually was busier than usual, which Lilly was thrilled about. She hurried from customer to customer, brewing tea samples, teaching about remedies, wrapping up sales and dispensing personal advice on occasion. She was still being sought out as an agony aunt. By eleven o'clock the shop was packed and Lilly was wondering how she was going to find time to replenish what she'd sold from the stock at the back, when a young blonde woman entered.

Lilly sized her up and came to the conclusion she was neither local nor English. She was of athletic build, slim, tanned and radiating health with hair tied in a high ponytail, wearing jeans, trainers and a white tee shirt under a faded raspberry hoodie advertising a well-known brand of soft drink. She returned Lilly's smile, showing perfectly straight and white teeth.

"Welcome to The Tea Emporium."

"Hey, thanks. You're Lilly Tweed, the owner, right?" The girl replied in an American accent.

"Yes, I am. Are you looking for anything in particular?"

"Oh, I'm not here to shop," she replied, thrusting an envelope into Lilly's hands.

Opening it, Lilly found an application. "Oh, you're looking for a job?"

"Sure am," she said, sticking out her hand and shaking Lilly's with a strong, confident grip. "My name's Stacey. Stacey Pepper. I just started at the university and am looking for something part time. You're looking to fill a part time position, right?"

With the sign in the window, Lilly could hardly say otherwise. "Yes. But do you know anything about tea, Stacey?"

"I know it's brewed in a kettle, but that's about it. I'm a quick learner, though."

"Actually, the tea is brewed in a teapot," Lilly gently corrected her with a smile. "The kettle is used for boiling the water, which is poured into the teapot."

"Right! I think it's an English versus American terminology thing. But don't worry, I won't forget again."

"Perhaps you're right. Well, I'll be sorting through the applications this evening and..."

"Oh, drat it!" a man's voice rang out just as the unmistakable sound of smashing china reached Lilly's ears.

ceiling

"LILLY, I AM so sorry," an elderly man said with a combined look of horror and shame. "Don't worry about it, Jeffrey. It was an accident."

"But that's twice in as many weeks! You must let me pay for it this time," he said, reaching for his wallet with a shaking hand.

"Honestly, it's not necessary," Lilly began.

"It is, you know. I insist."

While Lilly had been speaking with Jeffrey, Stacey had taken it upon herself to start picking up the bits of broken china.

"Stacey, be careful!" Lilly said. "I don't want you cutting yourself. I'll deal with it in a minute."

"I don't mind. Where's your mop and broom?"

Lilly sighed. "In the back storeroom, just behind the door, you'll find the dustpan and brush and a mop and bucket. Thank you."

While Stacey busied herself cleaning up the mess, Lilly rang Jeffrey's payment into the large antique till. Then she had an idea. A few days before, a company rep had come in and left some product samples with her. Now, normally Lilly didn't like plastic products, they were harmful to both the environment and the wildlife. All her merchandise was sold in paper bags or cardboard boxes. However, these she would make an exception for as they were recycled plastic. She dug one out of the box under the counter and set it in front of Jeffrey with a smile. A beautiful deep teal with a gold rim teacup and saucer, styled like its china counterparts. It was so perfectly put together that unless you knew, it was almost impossible to distinguish between it and the real deal.

Jeffrey shook his head. "I don't want to have another mishap, Lilly."

"You won't. I promise. Pick it up."

Jeffrey did so, then broke out in a huge grin. "Well, I never. Isn't that amazing? I would never have guessed."

"Would you like refill?"

"I would indeed. My usual please, Miss Tweed."

Lilly laughed and reached for the Fennel, known to help brain function. The first time he'd broken one of her cups, Jeffrey had confided that he'd been diagnosed with early onset Parkinson's disease. The tremors had caused him to lose his grip. There was little Lilly could do in the way of help, but Jeffrey was adamant the Fennel tea was alleviating his symptoms and who was she to question it?

With Jeffrey sorted out, Lilly made a note to order a few more of the plastic range of tea cups for her samples. They would be a lovely alternative for those elderly customers who had trouble gripping and lifting a heavier china version. It seemed Jeffrey had the same idea.

"I say, Lilly, do you sell this range? I'd love to have a set at home. Much more practical."

"It's something new I'm trying, so I can add your order to mine, Jeffrey. I'll have to confirm the price for you, but it shouldn't be too expensive."

He made a vague gesture with his hand, dismissing her concerns. "Whatever it is, it will be cheaper than constantly breaking and having to replace the china ones. Order me a set of six would you, my dear?"

By the time that was done, the mess was cleaned up, everything had been returned to the store room and Lilly had several other customers to serve. She had no idea what had happened to Stacey. Ten minutes later she got her answer as Stacey came over with arms full of merchandise she was carrying for a customer. The older woman was laughing at something the younger girl had said and thanking her profusely for her help.

"Anytime," Stacey replied.

She's acting as though she already works here, Lilly thought with amusement. For the next hour she didn't have time to think about the confident American girl. There were simply too many customers in the shop to deal with. She did notice that Stacey stood to one side, observing and making notes in a small notebook. She was obviously keen.

Shortly after lunch and with the shop now empty, Lilly had time to grant the girl a more formal interview. She brewed them both a cup of Rooibos, a red tea from South Africa, and took a seat at the far end of the counter.

"Well, you've certainly got my attention, Miss Pepper," Lilly began. "But what do you think qualifies you to work in my shop?"

"Honestly, not much. Although I am good with people. But I'm willing to learn like I said before. And I'm a quick study."

"And do you drink tea?"

"A bit, although nothing like the stuff you have here. My dad's actually a Brit, from London, but I've spent most of my life living with my mom in the US. I decided to apply to college here and was accepted. It'll give me a chance to get to know my dad better."

Lilly smiled and nodded but remained silent. She'd learned that if you kept quiet, people were inclined to fill the silence. It was a good way to get to know more, and Stacey obliged.

"My parents divorced when I was five," she continued. "Mom's old job meant she travelled a lot, it's how she met my dad. They lived in London for a while, but after the divorce she took me with her back to the States. Dad is pretty much a once a year call on my birthday kind of parent."

"I'm sorry, Stacey."

"Hey, it's no problem. We're cool. He was pretty pleased to have me move over here to go to school."

"Divorces can be nasty, though. I went through one myself a few years ago. It was fairly civil, but of course there were no children involved."

"Nah," Stacey said, waving Lilly's comments away. "As far as I know, they get along fine. Better now they aren't living together, actually."

"Well, that's positive at least," Lilly said just as Earl made an appearance and jumped straight into Stacey's lap.

"Hey there," she exclaimed, scratching his ears. "What's his name?"

"Earl."

"Earl, and he's grey. So, Earl Grey like the tea, right?"

Lilly nodded, pleased she had picked up on the intended pun.

"Cute. So, um... do you have any questions for me?"

"No, I don't think so. But you really were a great help today and Earl seems to like you."

Stacey grinned expectantly. "I love animals. So, you're considering me?"

"How about a trial run?"

"Awesome!"

"All right. I'll get some leaflets together for you to study on the types of tea I offer and their health benefits. We can discuss your hours once you've been through them. Do you have any other questions?"

"Only about that little letterbox out the front. I saw some of your customers using it and wondered what it was for?"

Lilly explained her former job as an agony aunt with the paper. That even though she no longer worked there, many people still wanted her advice and had taken to coming to the shop instead.

"Sometimes they come in to chat over tea, but others have problems which are more private, so I installed a letterbox outside. The letters drop into the basket inside and I collect them each day and take them home to answer them."

"Cool!" Stacey said. "I just love this place. I think I'm really going to enjoy working here."

Chapter Two

A COUPLE OF HOURS later the day was over and Lilly began the process of shutting the shop. She moved the signs and flowers from the bicycle display back inside and put Earl in his carrier. After taking out the day's takings and balancing the receipts, she transferred it all to the safe in the storeroom. It had been one of her best days so far. Not least she suspected because of Stacey and her way with the customers. She certainly knew how to sell.

Her last job was to remove that day's letters from her agony aunt basket. "Four today, Earl," she said to the cat. "Let's get home and see how we can help."

As she locked the door and put Earl in the bike basket, she felt the wind begin to rise. Dark clouds were beginning to roll in over the moor. "Looks like rain. We better get a move on otherwise we could be drenched before we get home."

Retracing the morning's route, Lilly was just at the end of the park when the first light drops of rain began to fall. They quickly turned into a deluge, soaking her to the skin and plastering her unruly hair to her face.

"Good grief," she said, picking up speed, eager to get out of the wet. "Where did this come from?" Earl, tucked up comfortably in his warm carrier, didn't respond.

Ten minutes later, she stopped outside her cottage gate. Snug in its cloak of trees with views over the river, it was part of the nature reserve a short distance North East of the town centre. An incredibly picturesque setting, even with the gloom of an impending storm. Leaving her bike in the shed, she retrieved the cat and dashed inside.

After she'd fed Earl, she put her dinner in the oven and went for a long hot shower while it cooked. An hour or so later, warm again and nicely full, Lilly settled down with a cup of chamomile tea and the agony aunt letters.

The first was from a local teenager discussing problems at school. Struggling with mounting responsibilities and social pressures, Lilly advised the youngster to confide in parents and teachers, or if that wasn't possible, at least discuss the issues with her friends, who were most likely in the same situation. She also recommended some books and on-line resources which would help. The main thing for her to understand was that she was not alone, and that there were always solutions to be found. She signed off by saying if the girl wanted to talk face to face at any time, then Lilly could be found at the shop.

The second was a brief note from a gentleman looking to start his own business. However, he had some concerns regarding the landlord of the building he wished to lease.

During her time at the paper Lilly had amassed a number of professional contacts, including someone at the local council who dealt with Landlord Registration in the locality. She also gave the name of a solicitor who could look over the lease. Her final piece of advice was to seek out and talk to the other tenants of this landlord and get their views.

The third note was simply a suggestion card. She kept them on the counter in the shop and used the letterbox outside to receive them. It helped keep the privacy of those with a genuine problem, as no one noticed who was posting what. She put it to one side and turned to the final letter, fully expecting it to be something simple to deal with. She was wrong.

*M*ISS TWEED, THE letter began.

> *You're my last hope. If you can't help me, then I don't know what I will do. I think I'm being followed and I'm frightened. My doctor says I'm paranoid, and it's part of my illness, but he's wrong. Someone has been in my home when I'm out and my husband is having an affair, I'm sure of it.*

"Oh, Earl, this poor woman."

Lilly put the letter down and rubbed her eyes. This was much more than she could deal with. She wasn't a doctor or a psychiatrist and had no official qualifications to call upon. The woman was obviously suffering some sort of mental health breakdown and needed professional help. The writing was messy and hurried, as though the author were trying to get everything down while they were lucid enough to remember it. It flitted from one statement to the next with no cohesion, and there were several wet splotches across the page too. Tears, Lilly thought sadly. The woman was in dreadful emotional pain. She picked up the letter and continued to read...

> *They say I'm imagining it all, but I've been taking my tablets, and it's still happening. I don't know what to do. Am I seeing things, Miss Tweed? It's hard to know what's real and what isn't when my senses have failed me so many times before. I know I've been a burden to those around me. Perhaps this is their way of getting rid of me for good? To make me think I am crazy after all. But I don't feel safe anywhere now, even in my own home.*
>
> *What shall I do, Miss Tweed? Can you help me? I don't know who else to turn to because I feel I can't trust anyone. They're all lying to me.*
>
> *Please write back.*
> *Carol Ann Hotch.*

Lilly made herself another cup of tea, the first forgotten about and now cold. Then settled down to write a reply to Carol Ann.

It took over an hour and several attempts before she was happy with what she had written. She finished off by saying she would be more than willing to meet with Carol Ann either at her home, the tea shop or any other place Carol Ann felt comfortable. She was not to think she was alone and without support. She wasn't. Lilly would help in any way she could.

Once finished, she gathered the three letters together and hopped on her bike to take them to the post box at the end of the lane. The final letter had been the most urgent one she'd ever received, and she wanted the reply to get there as soon as possible. The postman would pick up at seven-thirty the next morning, so Carol Ann should have her reply the day after. Lilly just hoped she'd agree to meet.

IT HAD BEEN three days since Stacey Pepper had waltzed into Lilly's shop and practically demanded a job, and Lilly was very pleased with how things were going. The day after she'd been sent home with the information leaflets, Stacey had returned having memorised most of it and promptly set about sampling the various teas in order to get a better handle on the tastes.

Day three and Lilly had the official paperwork for her employment together and work schedule sorted out. Stacey was assisting customers and even making recommendations, but if she was unsure, she always turned to Lilly for assistance. This was a big plus in the girl's favour as far as Lilly was concerned. Never be too proud to ask for help or conceited enough to think you know it all.

Without being told, Stacey had also changed her casual outfit for a smart white polo shirt and black trousers, similar to what Lilly herself wore. The long, black, bibbed aprons with The Tea Emporium logo on the front pocket in gold, finished off the look.

"I have to say I'm impressed," Lilly said as Stacey returned from helping a customer to her car with not one but two full tea services, and another on order.

"Really?" she replied, a huge grin on her face.

"Really," Lilly assured her. "I can't believe how much you've picked up in only three days. If I'm being honest, yesterday I thought you were just using it as an excuse to gorge yourself on all my tea samples before I saw your notebook."

Stacey laughed. "I wouldn't do that. But I need to know what they taste like to sell them."

"So what are your thoughts? Do you have a favourite?"

"I like a lot of them. I didn't realise tea could taste so great and be good for you. But I think my favourite is the Chamomile. It tastes like apples and honey."

"It does. Although the trick with that one is not to leave it steeping for too long otherwise it starts to taste bitter. And that reminds me, we're running short of both the chamomile and the ginger. Could you pop upstairs and get some more?"

"Upstairs?"

"Yes, there's a flat above. Just go out the back and there's the entrance door to the left." Lilly said, handing over the keys.

"I didn't realise you owned that too."

"It's just storage at the moment, but at some point the plan is to get it organised and rent it out."

"Hey, my organisation is great. If that's the goal, then I'm happy to make a start on the back storeroom. I think with a bit of rearranging I can fit a lot more back there."

"I might just take you up on that, Stacey. Thanks."

A few minutes after Stacey had left, Lilly spied a young man hovering outside the shop window. A student, she thought and was proved right when he turned and she spied the university logo on his sweatshirt. He looked exhausted. Unruly hair as though he'd just crawled out of bed. Dark circles under his eyes and a haunted look. She poured a cup of recently made peppermint tea, good for relieving stress, and took it out to him.

"Hi. Sorry, I didn't mean to make you jump. You look like you could use this."

He stared at her blankly for a moment, then took the cup with a smile.

"Thanks, that's kind of you. You're the owner, er, Lillian Tweed, is that right?"

"Yes, but call me Lilly. Lillian is my Sunday name."

"Yeah, I've got one of those too. Frederick. Frederick Warren, but known as Fred."

"Nice to meet you, Fred. Is there anything I can help with? I don't want to interfere of course if you're just window shopping."

"No I... well, actually a friend told me about your letter box. You helped her when she wrote to you and..."

"Do you want to come in, Fred? The shop's quiet at the moment."

He paused for a moment but eventually nodded and followed her in, clutching his tea cup and saucer as though his life depended on it.

❧

*L*ILLY TOOK FRED down to the far end of the counter away from any shop browsers and refilled his tea cup.

"I love your shop," Fred said. "Really vintage looking. It's like going back to the past."

"And that's exactly what I was aiming for. It seemed fitting, not only because of the age of the town and the building, but because tea has been used as a medicine for thousands of years."

"Wow. I didn't know that."

"There's a well known Chinese proverb which says, *'Drinking a daily cup of tea will surely starve the apothecary.'*"

"It looks a bit like an old chemist shop, actually."

Lilly smiled. She wouldn't push the boy to speak to her about personal matters if he didn't want to.

"It used to be. Well, you're welcome to stay as long as you want. Drink your tea and relax a bit. If you want to talk, I'm here. If not, that's fine too."

Lilly moved away and grabbing a tea towel began to dry the recently washed cups and saucers.

Fred cleared his throat, then suddenly blurted out, "My girlfriend's pregnant."

No wonder he looked as though he hadn't slept for a while. Doubtless he could see his future disappearing before his eyes.

"That must be very difficult for you, Fred. I expect it feels as though the world has just ended, doesn't it? But believe me, it hasn't. Things are never as bad as they first appear. There is always help. You've made the first step by coming here. Talking with someone else will give you clarity. Have you talked to your girlfriend about your feelings?"

He shook his head. "She doesn't know I've found out. I thought she would have told me, but she didn't. I don't know what to do."

"Well, she could be afraid to tell you. Have you been together long?"

"About a year."

"I can't tell you what to do, but I feel the first step would be to sit down and discuss it with her. You obviously care or you wouldn't be feeling so wretched about it."

"But it's not mine."

Ah, that shone a completely different light on it. Not only was he dealing with the shock of the pregnancy, but the heartbreak of finding out his long-term girlfriend had been with someone else.

"How can you be sure?"

"Because we've never... you know," Fred said, blushing furiously. "She wanted to wait, and I was fine about it. Obviously she just took me for an idiot."

"You don't know that for sure, Fred. How did you find out?"

"I found the pregnancy test in her dorm room bin. Positive. I thought it belonged to her house mate at first. Then she asked me to grab her phone from her bag one day and there were some, I don't know, vitamins I think. You know, for pregnant women."

Lilly nodded.

"She's had some doctor appointments recently and... well I couldn't keep denying it then, could I? I knew."

"I can't imagine how tough this must be for you, Fred. You've got some difficult decisions to make. Do you still want to be with her?"

"I thought I did, but now I'm not sure. I mean she cheated on me, which is bad enough, but she's carrying someone else's child. I'm twenty two, Miss Tweed, I don't..."

Fred's voice wobbled. He was close to tears.

"I understand, Fred. You don't have to explain it to me. But, if I can offer one word of advice, it's this: talk to her but be gentle, she'll be scared herself. It's no use waiting because it will just drag on and on otherwise, which isn't healthy for either of you. Tell her you know she's pregnant and probably scared and see what she has to say. And if you need to talk at anytime, you know where I am. Don't shoulder all this yourself, Fred, there's help and support if you know where to look."

He nodded, giving a wan smile. "Yeah. Thanks for listening, I appreciate it."

"Anytime. I mean it."

"Hey, can someone give me hand?" a muffled voice called from the store-room door.

Frederick jumped from his seat and hurried over to help Stacey with several boxes.

"Oh, thanks."

"No problem."

"Hey, you go to the university, right? I think I've seen you around the campus."

"Oh, yeah, you're the American. Um, Pepper or something?"

"Stacey Pepper. And you?"

"Fred Warren," he said politely. "Well, I have to go. Nice to meet you. Thanks for the tea, Miss Tweed."

"You're welcome, Fred," Lilly said as he left the shop.

"Was he here to buy tea?"

Lilly said nothing.

"Oh, I get it. He was consulting your alter ego. I won't ask any more. So, there were a few chamomile and ginger teas to choose from. I didn't know which one you meant, so I brought them all."

"Sorry, Stacey. It's these two I should have been more specific."

"No problem. I'll take these back upstairs."

"And after that, do you think you could use your organisational skills to get the back room in better shape?"

"Absolutely!"

Lilly was very pleased to note Stacey didn't push her for information about her consultation with Fred. As an agony aunt, she was privy to many secrets and people trusted her not to gossip. Thankfully, it looked as though Stacey was the same.

She looked up just as the bell above the door rang and a familiar face walked in.

"Archie Brown!" she exclaimed, pleased to see him. "I wondered when I'd get a visit from you."

"Sorry it's been so long, Lilly." He said, removing his Trilby hat and giving her a peck on the cheek. "It's a busy life as a crime reporter, you know."

"Have a seat and I'll get you a drink. What do you fancy?"

"Anything to take the edge off and stop me wanting to throw things."

Lilly raised an eyebrow. This was unlike the Archie she knew. She perused her tea selection then nodded, picking a passionflower blend noted for helping with stress. She chose Rooibos for herself and with both teas made she asked him how life at the newspaper had been since she'd left.

Archie sighed. "Awful, if I'm honest. Abigail Douglas, your replacement, is a complete nightmare. She's ruined your column and unfortunately has discovered people are still writing to you. She knows about your letterbox outside and she's on the war path, I'm afraid."

Chapter Three

"I REALISED THERE MUST be a problem when the column was missing from the paper, but it's hardly my fault. I installed the letterbox because I was getting so many letters. I thought it would trickle off once they got used to Abigail. Looks like that's not going to be the case though, doesn't it?"

Archie scoffed. "Well, it's hardly surprising considering she's unintentionally 'outed' a couple of people in the column already. Infidelity and fraud, would you believe? Didn't go as far as actually naming them, but gave enough clues so that they'd be recognised by their nearest and dearest. People won't write in to her if she's going to splash their problems all over the paper."

"But she can't do that, Archie! Doesn't she realise this is a small town? You can't walk six feet without bumping into someone you know."

Lilly broke off for a moment to serve a couple of customers who had come in for their regular supplies.

"Try telling Abigail that," Archie continued once Lilly had returned. "She's from a bigger concern, remember. Dealing with large cities where people don't know their neighbours and sensationalism sells papers. Her advice is dreadful. She's peddling gossip rather than genuine advice. Between you and me, I think she wrote the last few herself. But don't repeat that."

"Of course I won't. So, if the column is failing, what's she doing?"

"She's after my job."

"What? I saw the article about the thefts at the University, but I thought she was just covering because you were so busy."

"Oh no. She went behind my back. Unbelievable isn't it. Apparently the agony aunt thing was just to get her foot in the door. She's always wanted to be a crime reporter. Says she's got *unique skills*, whatever that means, and fully expects to win awards and have the nationals fighting to give her a job. She's completely delusional if you ask me. She can't get a decent quote anywhere because no one will talk to her, so she exaggerates."

"I'm sorry, Archie. Is there anything I can do to help?"

"See, that's why I'm here. For a bit of tea and sympathy."

Lilly laughed. "You know, that would have been a great name for the shop."

"And talking of the shop... you've done a superb job here, you know. I'm so pleased you were able to put the redundancy money to good use. I don't know why I felt so worried for you. You've got a knack for bouncing back."

"I've had a lot of support from the community though, Archie. The place wouldn't have worked without them."

"Don't sell yourself short, Lilly. There's a reason you've got their support. You're a good person and they like you. You give sound advice and never gossip. Plus, your tea is excellent." He said, draining his cup.

"Do you want a re-fill?"

"Yes, but I'd better not. Look, there's another reason I dropped in."

"Oh?" Lilly questioned, raising an eyebrow. Archie's expression had changed. She'd seen that look before when he was working on a serious article. "What's happened?"

"It's not common knowledge yet." Archie leaned closer, his voice dropping to a whisper. "But there's a body been found in the river."

Lilly gasped. "A body?"

Archie nodded. "I've a contact at the police station, as you know. The body of a woman was found early this morning by a couple of joggers."

"What happened?"

Archie shrugged. "It could have been an accident, or maybe suicide. I don't have much information at the moment. I expect the autopsy will be done over the next few days and we'll know more then. But be prepared for a possible visit from the authorities. I wanted to be the one to tell you first."

"Me? But why would they want to see me? Wait, was it someone I know?" A nervous knot had formed in her stomach and she suddenly shivered.

"I assume so. There was a letter from you found in her pocket."

LILLY COULDN'T HELP but breathe a sigh of relief. "Someone needing advice, then? Do you have a name?"

"Carol Ann something. Hang on..." he said, fishing in his pocket for his notebook.

"Hotch." Lilly finished for him.

"Yes, that's right. You do know her then?"

"No. I never met her but I won't forget her name in a hurry. She wrote to me asking for help and naturally I wrote back. It was a really alarming letter, Archie. The poor woman was convinced she was being followed. That someone was breaking into her home. She was frightened for her safety but was told she was being paranoid. Now she's dead."

"The police are aware she had mental health issues, but I can't get anyone to talk just yet. Reading between the lines, I believe they're thinking it's either an accidental or deliberate overdose of her medication. Of course until we get the post-mortem results back it's all speculation."

"Do you think she would have written to me asking for help if she was planning to commit suicide?"

Archie sat back, arms folded while he thought. "Undoubtedly it does seem odd," he said finally. "But by the same token, she obviously wasn't in her right mind. I've yet to speak to the husband but according to my contact he's been worried something like this was going to happen for a while."

Lilly got up to brew herself another cup of tea. Passionflower for herself too, this time. She was feeling twitchy and anxious as a result of Archie's news.

"I feel dreadful," she said. "I should have reported her letter to the proper authorities, rather than write asking her to meet then waiting for a response."

"Lilly, you can't blame yourself for what happened," Archie said sternly. "Thinking that way is ridiculous. You'll make yourself ill. You did the only thing you could."

"I don't even know what she looked like. I could have passed her in the street. She could even have been in here and I wouldn't have known."

"Well, I can help with that." Archie reached into his coat pocket and withdrew a photograph. "A copy from my friendly police officer."

Lilly took the image. Staring back at her was a youngish attractive woman with shining strawberry blond hair, holding a small white dog. A Pomeranian, she thought. She looked happy and content. Without a care in the world. She didn't look like someone so unhappy with life that they wanted to end it. But then depression was a hidden disease. Appearances could be deceiving, and this was nothing but a single snapshot of her life. She quickly took a photo with her phone and offered the original back to Archie.

"No, it's fine. You keep it, I've got another."

"Hello," said a voice behind them.

"Oh, Stacey. I didn't hear you there. Archie, this is Stacey Pepper. She's just started working with me. Stacey, this is Archie Brown, head crime reporter with The Plumpton Mallet Gazette."

"Nice to meet you, Archie. Are you here for some tea? We have something for every occasion and most ailments you know. This one for example..."

31

Lilly smiled at how easily Stacey had turned the conversation to business and listened as she explained in detail the various teas and their health properties. Archie looked at her briefly and grinned, but played along, asking sensible questions with a keen interest. Having worked with Lilly for so long previously, he knew almost as much about tea as she did, but understood this was important to Stacey.

While the discussion continued, Lilly tuned out and turned back to the photograph of Carol Ann Hotch. *Something isn't right,* she thought. *I understand the assumption that it was accidental. It might very well have been, but I can't see a woman taking her own life so soon after writing to me so desperate for help.*

She sighed and put the photo back in her pocket. There were customers to serve. But as the working day drew to a close, the nagging doubt wouldn't leave her. She had an inexplicable feeling something was dreadfully wrong.

*L*ILLY HAD ALREADY sent Stacey home as she had a test to study for and was in the process of closing up when there was an almighty crash of thunder which rattled the windows and the heavens opened. Great sheets of rain poured down from the awning above the shop as the storm took hold, producing a waterfall so dense you couldn't see the square beyond. Luckily, she'd already brought in her bike and the plants.

"Right, Earl, it looks as though we're getting a taxi home. I have no intention of cycling in this."

Earl was weaving a figure eight around her legs, so she scooped him up and put him in his carrier. With a final check, she grabbed her coat and exited through the back door where she'd arranged for the taxi driver to pick her up. To her surprise, she spotted Stacey in the main town car park, which was behind the shop, her head under the rear of the vehicle. It was an old Beetle which had definitely seen better days. In places, the original blue paint work had worn down to the metal.

"Stacey!" Lilly shouted through the wind.

Stacey looked up and seeing Lilly, slammed the boot, locked the car and rushed over.

"Hey."

"What are you still doing here? I thought you'd gone home ages ago."

"My car won't start. I thought I could fix it, but I'm clearly no mechanic. Serves me right for picking up the cheapest ride I could find. Didn't even have the decency to break down when the sun was shining."

Lilly laughed. "Well, I've just called a taxi. There was no way I was cycling home in this downpour; Earl would never have forgiven me. You can share it."

"That would be wonderful. Thanks so much. Oh, here it is, right on time."

The driver pulled up as close as he could and the two women jumped in the back seat, Earl between them. "Crazy weather," the driver said.

"You're telling me," Stacey replied. Peeling layers of wet hair from her face.

"So, where to, ladies?"

"We'll get you home first, Stacey," Lilly said. "You're soaked to the skin."

Stacey hesitated slightly. "It's okay. You probably live closer than I do."

"I insist." Lilly didn't know the girl well but as her employer she felt responsible.

Stacey gave the driver her address and Lilly then understood her initial reticence. The area was on the outskirts of the town, the less salubrious part made up of cheap accommodation and the odd shop rapidly going out of business.

Once they'd arrived, Stacey fumbled in her purse for her part of the fare, but Lilly said no, it was on her. At that moment Earl chose to be sick.

"Oh, Earl, you poor thing. What's caused that? Is it the storm? Stacey, would you mind if I brought him in to clean up?"

"Sure, no problem."

Lilly paid the taxi driver, and they both hurried over to the building Stacey called home. Originally it would have been a large single townhouse, but the planners in their wisdom had decided that making it into four cramped flats was a good idea. Stacey's was on the top floor at the back, under the eaves.

While the young girl went to change out of her wet clothes, Lilly released Earl and filled a bowl of water for him. Then cleaned the carrier, leaving it on the draining board to dry. While she waited for Stacey, Lilly observed her surroundings with dismay. The flat was in an awful state. Wallpaper that looked as though it had last been in fashion in the mid sixties was peeling away from the walls. There were signs of mould in the upper corners and in several places water was leaking in from the roof and Stacey had laid out various pots and pans to catch the drips. Unfortunately, due to the storm raging outside, they were currently mini waterfalls. It was damp and unattractive, although Stacey had tried to liven it up a bit with plants.

"Sorry about the state of the place," Stacey said when she returned. "It's temporary. I needed somewhere close to school, and this was the first place that was available."

"It's not you who should be apologising, Stacey, it's your landlord. At the very least, the roof needs fixing."

"It only leaks when it rains," Stacey replied with a grin.

"I have news for you. This is England. It rains a lot. Have you told your landlord how bad it is?"

"Yep. I've emailed pictures and videos, too. She says she'll get it sorted as soon as her builder has some time. But honestly, I'm planning to get out as soon as I can. It's one of the reasons I pushed so hard for the job. I want to get somewhere closer to town."

Stacey made a pot of coffee and they sat at the small Formica-topped table while Earl curled up on an easy chair nearby.

"Do you think your father could help you with a better place to live?"

"I've only spoken to him once since I arrived in England." She said sadly.

Lilly could tell there was more to the story but didn't want to push too much.

"Oh, has he been busy?"

Stacey shrugged. "I don't know. Actually, I don't know my dad at all, really. I told you I came here to get to know him better, and that's true. But... it wasn't exactly part of his plans."

"He didn't know you were coming to England?"

"He knew. I don't think it was something he wanted, though. I think he was pretty content with things the way they were; namely me being a million miles away and him sending a card with money in once or twice a year. When I told him my plans we talked on the phone some, but he didn't seem all that eager to get together. So, to answer your first question, no, I don't think dear old dad would help me with a better apartment."

"I'm sorry, Stacey."

"Hey, no worries. I have an awesome stepfather. A great role model actually, and he really loves me and my mom. I was just hoping dad would be a bit more excited that I was here. But, whatever. His loss, right? I'm here to get my degree. That's the important thing."

"Good for you," Lilly said, finishing off her coffee. "You know, if you want more hours at the shop..."

"Yes," Stacey said quickly. "I definitely want more hours at the shop. As long as it doesn't interfere with school, I'll take as many hours as you can give me."

"Wonderful. I'm sure we'll work something out that suits us both. In the meantime, do you think you'd be okay opening up on your own tomorrow?"

"Definitely! You can count on me." She said taking the keys from Lilly.

They chatted a bit longer, then Lilly lifted a sleeping Earl and put him in the now dry carrier. By the time she got back outside the taxi she'd called was already waiting and half an hour later she was back in the warmth of her own cottage.

Setting the table for dinner, she was in the process of collecting up the agony aunt letters to transfer to her files, when she spotted the one from Carol Ann Hotch on the top. Regardless of what Archie had said, she still felt partially guilty at not being able to help the woman before it was too late. Then she saw something she'd missed previously. On the reverse of the paper, discreetly printed at the bottom, was a business address for *Dr. Jorgenson. MD. Psychiatrist.*

"That must be her doctor, Earl." Lilly said to the disinterested cat.

A quick on-line search revealed the office wasn't far from the centre of Plumpton Mallet, on one of the side streets. It was also open for another twenty minutes. A quick phone call later and she had an appointment set up for the following morning.

"What?" Lilly asked the cat who was staring straight at her. "Don't look at me like that, Earl. I just want a few answers to set my mind at rest, that's all."

Earl stalked away, tail held high. Lilly swore he shook his head at her in disgust.

Chapter Four

THE NEXT MORNING Lilly woke with a start, thinking she'd overslept as the sunlight poured in through the curtains. Then, remembering Stacey was opening up, she sank back into her pillow with a sigh of relief hoping for a rare lie in. The rest was short-lived, however, because a moment later Earl jumped up on the bed and started meowing in her ear. It was obviously time for breakfast.

Once she was ready to leave, Lilly momentarily contemplated leaving Earl at home. At a good clip, it was at least a half an hour walk to The Tea Emporium, and she didn't really want to take her car as it was such a lovely day. But Earl was much happier at the shop with people, and she'd never left him alone before. So putting him in his carrier, she took him with her.

Arriving at the market square, Lilly was pleased to note Stacey had set the bike outside and decorated it as she herself did. Inside there were several customers, some browsing, a couple with baskets full of merchandise and one looking through a catalogue with Stacey trying to choose a tea set.

Lilly opened the carrier and released Earl, who gave a languorous stretch before occupying his bed in the window.

"Good morning, Mrs Erickson," Lilly said as she passed Stacey and the woman she was helping.

"Oh, Lilly, there you are. I was surprised not to see you this morning. But don't worry, Stacey has been a great help. She's helping me find a tea set for my daughter-in-law. And I think we've found the perfect one."

Lilly gave Stacey a wink. "Well, that's excellent news, Mrs Erickson. Stacey has a very good eye when it comes to the china and is very knowledgeable about the teas."

"Oh, she's a credit to you, that's for sure."

Lilly made her way to the till to serve those wishing to buy, but with that done, for the first time since she'd opened the shop she found herself with little to do. Checking the vintage train station clock on the exposed brick wall opposite, she decided she may as well set off for her appointment. It would be better to take a leisurely stroll and arrive a little early. Once Stacey was free, she explained her plans.

"No problem, I can manage here."

"You've done an excellent job here this morning, Stacey. Thank you. I shouldn't be more than a couple of hours, but I'll have my phone if you need me. I'll pick us up some lunch on the way back."

Stacey grinned. "Sounds good to me. Thanks, Lilly."

The spring sunshine had brought both locals and tourists out in their droves, and the town centre was awash with people shopping, chatting with friends and soaking up the warmth while having coffee and pastries at the pavement cafes. Because of the shop and her former job, Lilly was well known in Plumpton Mallet and spoke to several people on her way through the square. Stopping to chat briefly with her fellow shop owners who were making the most of the weather by either, cleaning front windows, hanging their flower baskets or sweeping the broad pavement. There was a distinct holiday buzz about the place, and Lilly found herself walking with a spring in her step as she approached the doctor's office.

On the wall outside the double story building was a discreet brass plaque; *Dr Jorgenson MD*, the same as the notepaper on which Carol Ann had scrawled her letter. Inside, contrary to the hustle and bustle she'd just walked through, was an oasis of calm. Peaceful, with warmly upholstered furniture, deep pile rugs and several large potted ferns. Comfortable chairs were positioned around an unlit but working Victorian fireplace, and on a half moon console table in the side alcove a tinkling water feature was displayed. Occasional tables sported a variety of magazines, and a discreet rack was filled with leaflets advertising various support services.

Lilly approached the desk where a secretary was busy at a computer.

"Hello, may I help you?"

"Yes, I have an appointment. Lilly Tweed, I telephoned yesterday."

"Yes, of course. One moment." She reached into a drawer and handed Lilly some new patient paperwork to complete.

"If you'd like to take a seat, the Doctor will be with you shortly."

Lilly sat down and filled out the paperwork, secretly wondering how much a single session was going to cost considering her appointment was a ruse. She'd just signed and dated the final sheet when a smart but casually dressed man appeared. "Miss Tweed?" he asked politely as she stood up.

"Yes, that's right."

"I'm, Dr Jorgenson. You can leave your paperwork with Sarah. Come on through."

Lilly took a deep breath. There was no going back now. Fingers crossed the doctor wouldn't be angry at her subterfuge.

AKING A SEAT in a comfortable, warm office which was as well appointed as the reception area, Lilly observed the doctor. He looked to be in his mid-forties, the same as her, with a shock of blond hair. A legacy of his Nordic heritage, she thought, judging from his name. He spoke with no discernible foreign accent, so she assumed he was several generations removed from the original Viking settlers. He took a seat opposite, pen and notepad poised on his lap.

"So, what brings you here today, Miss Tweed?" he asked kindly. "Perhaps you could start by telling me a little about yourself?"

Lilly returned the smile. "Well, I've lived here all my life. I used to work for the local paper but now run The Tea Emporium in the market square."

"Do you know, I thought I recognised your name. You used to be the gazette's agony aunt, is that right?"

"Yes, it is. In your line of work I don't suppose you agree with agony aunts, do you?"

"On the contrary. I believe there's a place for them providing you're not attempting to diagnose or treat serious illness. That's my job," he said with a smile. "I used to read your column as a matter of fact, professional interest you understand, and found it to be honest and frank with good advice. I also happen to know if you came across something you weren't able to deal with, you'd advise the writer to seek professional help."

"Oh?" Lilly said, surprised he seemed to know so much about her.

"A couple of the doctors at the local health centre are friends of mine," he said by way of explanation. "Sadly, I can't say the same for the woman who took over from over you. I'm surprised people are still writing in."

Lilly nodded. "Actually, that's really the reason I'm here. Not actually for myself. When I left the paper, I found people still writing to me. So much so in fact that I installed a letterbox at the shop for that purpose. I got one very recently that disturbed me greatly and discovered it was written on the reverse of your surgery note paper. I naturally assumed she was one of your patients?" She reached into her pocket and pulled out the letter, passing it to Dr Jorgenson.

He took his glasses from his top shirt pocket and read the letter. "Oh dear. Yes, she is one of mine. I've been working with her for a number of years and thought she was doing well. This letter seems to suggest she may have relapsed. I have an appointment with her next week, but in light of this I think I'll ask Sarah to move it forward. Thank you for bringing it to me."

Lilly realised he had no idea his patient had died. And now it was suddenly up to her to break the bad news.

"*D*R JORGENSON, I am so sorry, but Carol Ann is dead. She was found drowned in the river yesterday."

She'd definitely taken him by surprise. He stared at her slack jawed and wide eyed for a moment, then said, "Are you sure?"

"I'm afraid so. I have a reporter friend at the paper who came and told me. My reply to her letter was found in her pocket, you see. I assumed the police had already been to talk to you."

"No. No, I haven't heard a thing. Although I expect they will turn up at some point. Was it an accident do you know?"

"Possibly, although the police think it may also have been suicide," Lilly answered. "I was curious about whether you believed she would take her own life having treated her? I mean, you must have known her better than anyone I would have thought. Was she suicidal?"

"Doctor-patient confidentiality doesn't allow me to discuss Carol Ann with you, Miss Tweed."

"I think someone killed her," Lilly blurted out, much to her own surprise as the doctor's.

"I beg your pardon? Why do you think that?"

"Read her letter again. She was afraid for her life. Regardless of whether or not her fears were justified, she certainly didn't want to die. Why would she write to me in fear one minute and pleading for my help, then take her own life so soon afterwards? It doesn't make sense to me."

Dr Jorgenson got up and poured a glass of water from the crystal carafe on the sideboard. Lilly declined one when asked.

"What exactly is your interest in Carol Ann, that you felt it necessary to seek out and schedule an appointment with me, her therapist?"

Lilly sat back and sighed heavily. "Honestly? I feel guilty and somehow responsible. I feel as though I should have done something more than just write back asking her to meet with me. I should have reported her letter, or gone to find her. Perhaps if I'd done more I could have prevented her death?"

"Assuming you're not the guilty party and I'm sure you're not, that would have taken some foreknowledge of the crime. You're obviously perceptive, but I don't think you're clairvoyant, Miss Tweed. Perhaps it would be wise to schedule an appointment for yourself after all."

Lilly smiled grimly, unsure whether he was being serious. "Maybe."

"Look, I shouldn't discuss a patient with you, there are obligations with regard to confidentiality, ethical more than legal now that she is deceased, but I don't want you blaming yourself. If it sets your mind at ease, Carol Ann was a very disturbed individual."

"So you do think it was suicide?"

"If not an accident, which I think the more likely, then yes, it's possible. She'd been diagnosed with paranoid schizophrenia many years ago, long before she became my patient, that's common knowledge. And I concurred with the findings of my colleague. It's a complicated illness and one where rational thought is absent a lot of the time."

"But she was obviously afraid of something, or someone. Do you know what or who it was?"

"To be honest, it would depend on what day you asked her. But there was a recurring name mentioned; Monica."

"Who is Monica?"

"I'm not actually certain she exists at all, Miss Tweed. When her name first came up I asked her husband about it. He said they had met someone of that name at a function quite a while ago but had never socialised together again after that. It seems Carol Ann may have created a fictitious person in her mind, a nemesis if you like, but given her a name of someone she had met in real life. It was a delusion I was working through with her."

"Thank you for telling me. I know you didn't have to."

"I hope it makes you feel less responsible for what happened."

"I still feel unsettled about the whole thing," Lilly admitted. "Moreover, I don't believe she took her own life. But perhaps it *was* nothing more than a simple accident."

"Let's hope so, Miss Tweed. The alternative doesn't bear thinking about. Now, you've still got," he looked at his watch.

"Twenty-five minutes of your session left. Perhaps there's something I can help you with personally?"

AFTER LEAVING DR Jorgenson's office Lilly was surprised to find herself feeling a bit better, in terms of her own involvement, regarding what happened to Carol Ann. It had, despite her insistence to herself that it would not, turned into a therapy session. Dr Jorgenson had a deep and soft melodious voice which had a definite soporific effect. She'd found herself relaxed, a rare occurrence, and comfortably discussing things she hadn't thought of in years. They'd spoken of her recent job loss and the risk she'd taken opening the shop. Her worry that it may not continue once the novelty had worn off. They'd even touched on the subject of her divorce nine years prior. It had been an amicable split, but there were aspects of it, which she hadn't fully admitted to herself, that bothered her even now. "Crikey, he's good," she muttered to herself as she left the premises. While she didn't see herself returning for any more therapy sessions, having reached a point in her life where she felt reasonably content and confident, she believed she had made a new friend of sorts in Dr Jorgenson.

Back in the market square Lilly stopped at her favourite bakery and cafe for two baguette sandwiches and some caramel slices for lunch, then returned to the shop where Stacey was, once again, handling things as though she had worked in the shop for years rather than just a matter of days.

"Lunch is served, Stacey," Lilly said, handing her the paper bag. "Just pop mine in the fridge, will you? I'll take my break when you're finished."

"Thanks, I'm so hungry. Are you sure you don't want to eat first?"

"No, you go ahead. You've earned it."

While Stacey was at lunch, Lilly busied herself with serving customers and restocking items which had sold. When it was her turn to eat, she had an idea.

After her appointment with Dr Jorgenson, the one thing which had stuck in her mind was the name Monica. While the doctor was inclined to believe she was a figment of Carol Ann's imagination, Lilly wanted to prove it one way or another and a good place to start was on-line. Almost everybody had a social media presence nowadays and after a bit of searching Lilly found not Carol Ann herself, but her husband, Joseph Hotch. It seemed he used his page primarily for professional purposes and shortly after she'd sent a friend request it was approved. This allowed her to look at his friend's list.

While not a very common name, she did find three people with the name Monica and set about searching each one individually, looking for the most likely candidate. Joseph Hotch was an architect, and his posts on the subject garnered quite a lot of interest. Two of the women had shared and commented, but there was no level of personal detail that would suggest they knew him socially. The third, however, a young woman named Monica Morris, lived locally and had commented on several of his personal posts. She was a university student, studying chemistry, and was a member of the college hockey team. If the Monica character that Carol

Ann had mentioned to Dr Jorgenson was in fact a real person, then it seemed likely this was the one.

She decided to pay a visit.

Chapter Five

"STACEY, I'VE GOT to pop out again. Will you be all right for a couple of hours?"

"Sure, no problem."

"Well, I've got..."

"Your phone if I need you?"

Lilly laughed. "Right. I'm obviously sounding like a broken record."

St John's university was a lengthy journey from the shop, so Lilly took her bike and cycled home to fetch her car. She only used it in foul weather these days or when she had a large shop to do, preferring to either walk or cycle, but the older model Mini Cooper painted in racing green, while not modern and a bit of a rattler was still reliable.

Twenty minutes later she parked in the university car-park and was walking across the tarmac to the principal building when she heard a voice calling her name. Her stomach sank.

"Abigail," she muttered. She'd only met the woman once when she handed over her job at the paper, but she'd recognise that grating voice anywhere. It was like fingernails on a blackboard. She turned and almost laughed.

Abigail was dressed in a knee-length white trench coat, tightly belted with the collar turned up, and high heeled black boots reaching up to her knees. But the cherry on top was the black fedora set at a rakish angle over hair which had been back combed to within an inch of its life. She was older than Lilly and, it had to be said, looked perfectly ridiculous. Archie was right she was after his job. But unlike Archie, she obviously felt that dressing like a female Sam Spade would automatically turn her into an investigative reporter.

"I thought that was you, Lillian."

"Hello, Abigail. How are things?"

"Well, I was going to say I can't complain. But actually I can. It's about that agony aunt letter box outside your shop. I want you to remove it. It's not your job now, dear, it's mine and you're making things difficult."

It wasn't just the ludicrous demand that astounded Lilly, but the condescending tone in which she spoke. Especially when she referred to her as 'dear.'

"I'm afraid I can't do that, Abigail. People are still writing to me for advice. But if they stop, then I'll be happy to remove it. I'm sure you agree that's fair?"

There wasn't much Abigail could say to that. But she was the sort of person who had to have the last word. "We'll see, dear. But I suppose we should bury the hatchet. I so dislike unpleasantness."

Hatchet? What hatchet? Thought Lilly. *I didn't realise there was a hatchet to bury.*

"Right. Well, anyway, if you'll excuse me, Abigail, I have to get on."

"I'll walk with you, dear. It appears we're going in the same direction."

Lilly sighed inwardly. She really could do without Abigail trailing after her. Then she had a sickening thought.

"What exactly are you doing here?"

Abigail smirked. "Hot on the trail of a clue, Lillian. I expect you already know about the body that was found? Yes, I thought you would. Anyway, I think I've found a connection between the dead woman and the university. So what do you say to that?"

"You're doing investigative journalism now?"

This wasn't quite the response Abigail had been expecting, but she gamely carried on. "Yes, of course. Being an agony aunt is rather demeaning when you have high skills elsewhere. I really should play to my strengths."

Lilly gritted her teeth. Had Abigail really no idea she'd just insulted her?

"So, Lillian, what are you doing here? Come to sell your tea in the staff canteen?"

Good grief, was there no end to the woman's vitriol? "Actually, I'm here for the same reason as you. I too found a connection between the university and the deceased woman."

Abigail stopped walking. "What? You're not a journalist. You don't even work for the paper anymore. So what do you think you are doing investigating?"

Lilly paused, wondering how much she should tell Abigail. But then again, she didn't actually know very much at all. She was here on a whim due to a gut feeling that something was amiss. She wanted to satisfy her curiosity more than anything and put to rest the uneasy feeling that she could have done something to prevent the woman's death. She wasn't really investigating; she had no experience with that sort of thing anyway. Abigail, however, did at least work for the paper and obviously something had brought her here. So, what harm could it do to be truthful with her? She took a deep breath and, although it might come back to bite her, decided to share what she knew.

"I feel somewhat responsible. You see, Carol Ann wrote to me asking for help a few days before she was found in the river. She was very upset and distressed and... Wait a minute. If you're here, you can't think it was an accident or suicide either. You're certainly not here to write an obituary. Am I right? What made you think it's something suspicious?"

Abigail blushed and shrugged. "Reporter's intuition, I suppose. I always did have a good nose for a story."

"Rubbish! What do you know?"

"Well, how charming!" Abigail said crossly, folding her arms in defence. "Fine, if you really want to know, I met her in the waiting room at Dr Jorgenson's. He's my therapist. I spoke to the woman a few times, and while completely off her rocker, I don't believe she was suicidal. Happy now?"

Lilly softened her tone slightly. "Were you and Carol Ann friends?"

52

"No, of course we weren't. What a ludicrous suggestion. The woman was as mad as a box of frogs. But, I swear, if you tell anyone I've been going to therapy..."

"You're not the only one who has therapy, Abigail. Millions of people benefit from having someone to talk to, particularly a stranger. It's much easier with a qualified professional than family or friends. You should know that being an agony aunt. As a matter of fact I was there myself only this morning."

"Oh, really? I see. Well, never mind that. I really must insist you leave the investigation to me, Lillian. You're not cut out for this line of work. Please, leave it to the expert." And with that parting shot, she began to stalk away.

Lilly called out to her retreating back. "If you're worried I'm going to step on your toes, or heaven forbid, beat you to the punch, don't be. I have no intention of writing an article independently and sending it to the Gazette. Although I could if I was so inclined." She added belligerently. It was a childish retort, but the woman had really got her back up.

Abigail rounded on her so fast she nearly lost her ridiculous hat. Lilly took a step back in surprise as the furious woman strode towards her, jabbing a finger in her face.

"You know there was a reason you were let go from the paper and replaced, Lillian Tweed," she hissed. "Professionalism. A real professional would have done something about that letter you received from Carol Ann. What did you do, exactly? If only she had written to me instead, then she... Well, I think you get the point. Stop meddling where you don't belong."

Lilly felt as though Abigail had punched her in the stomach. How dare she! Okay, it was nothing she hadn't already berated herself about, but she took exception to hearing it spewed forth in such a venomous and derogatory way. She was just on the verge of retaliating when they were interrupted.

"Is everything all right over here?" the voice of a young man asked. In Lilly's anger, she almost didn't recognise him. It was Frederick Warren, the student she'd helped at the shop earlier in the week.

"Thank you for your concern, young man. I'm afraid this lady was becoming hostile with me, but it's nothing I can't handle myself. You can be on your way." Abigail replied, with a dismissive wave of her hand.

Fred glanced quickly at Lilly, then back at Abigail.

"No, it's all right I'll stay."

"Young man, you are obviously too obtuse to take a hint so I will spell it out for you. We were having a private conversation. Go back to class."

"Actually, I think I'll stick around. My classes have finished for the day."

"Well, how rude! Who do you think you are?"

"Frederick Warren," he said with a grin. "I'm not bothering anybody by being here. I'm not bothering you, am I, Miss Tweed?"

"Not at all, Fred."

"Oh, for heaven's sake. So you know each other. Very amusing." And with that, Abigail stormed off.

Lilly laughed. "Thanks for rescuing me, Fred."

"No problem. What was that all about if you don't mind me asking? It seemed pretty heated."

"Nothing much. She blows hot and cold and thinks I want her job, which is nonsense."

"She's a bit of a tartar, isn't she?"

"Good grief, Fred, where did you hear an old fashioned word like that?"

Fred shrugged. "It was a favourite of my Gran's. I never really understood what it meant until now."

Lilly laughed. "Well, it's a favourite of mine again now, too. So, how are things with you, Fred?"

"Better, actually. I took your advice and my girlfriend, well ex-girlfriend now, had a long talk."

"So, you broke up?"

"Yeah, it was necessary, and we both agreed it was for the best. I was kind and supportive like you suggested, and I think she really appreciated it. I did tell her I thought she should talk to the baby's father as soon as possible. I'm not one-hundred percent sure, but I don't think he knows she's pregnant yet."

"Well done, Fred. You should be proud of yourself."

Fred shrugged. "So what are you doing here?"

"Just visiting, nothing exciting."

"Okay. Well, I better get to class or I'll be late."

"I thought your classes were finished for the day?"

"No. A little white lie. I didn't want to leave you on your own with that woman."

"Nicely done. Thank you, Fred. Tea's on me next time you're in town."

"You're on!"

She watched as Fred sped off to his class, wondering at his ability to lie so easily and convincingly, then made her way toward the main building. It was time to find Monica Morris. Preferably without bumping into Abigail again.

(decorative divider)

L ILLY DIDN'T KNOW where to start in her search for Monica, but as luck would have it, one of her regular patrons at the shop was in the reception area carrying an official looking clipboard as she entered.

"Hello, Janet. I didn't know you worked here, I thought you'd retired?"

"Hello, Lilly. You're a long way from town. Yes, I'm one of the administrators. Been here for, oh, it must be going on four years now. I found retirement didn't really suit me once I'd lost Reg. Not enough to do to fill in the days. I was a student here many moons ago, and when the job came up, I decided to apply. I didn't expect to get it, of course, but was thrilled when I did. It's been a Godsend quite frankly. So, are you wanting help with something?"

"I'm looking for a student, actually. She's a member of the hockey team if that's any help?"

"I assume she's written to you for advice? We do have a qualified counsellor on the faculty but of course some students prefer to seek outside help."

Although she felt a tad guilty, Lilly didn't put her right.

"I can't tell you where a specific student might be, but the girl's hockey team are all housed in G-Block. Just follow the path round the side of this building and it's directly behind. Someone there should be able to help you."

"Thanks, Janet. Pop into the shop sometime, I've a new blend of Oolong I think you might like."

"Lovely. I'll do that, I'm almost out of my usual blend. Would you mind signing in before you go to G-Block, Lilly? Anyone who is visiting is supposed to do so at reception."

"Oh, are they? No, of course I don't mind."

Lilly followed Janet to the reception desk where she signed the visitor's book, giving her name, the date and time. She listed her reason for visiting as seeing a student resident in G block on a private matter, which Janet authorised by co-signing. Tellingly, Abigail had not yet signed in.

She then exited the building and followed Janet's directions. Five minutes later she found herself outside G-Block. Jogging up the stone steps, she opened the main door and only narrowly avoided being knocked over by a short girl carrying a tall box.

"Gosh, I'm so sorry. I didn't see you. Can't see much of anything actually," she giggled.

"Don't worry, you missed me," Lilly said, taking in the hive of activity inside. "Are you getting ready for a party?"

"Yes. The ten-year reunion for past students. It's chaos as normal, but it usually works out all right in the end. Are you an old student?"

"Actually, Janet in admin just sent me over. I'm looking for Monica Morris?"

"Oh, right. She's in the common room. Just through that door over there," she indicated with a toss of her head. "She's the one in charge so you can't miss her."

"Thank you."

The common room was huge, at least the size of a tennis court, Lilly thought. With sofas and easy chairs arranged around tables and shelves full of books and board games. A television was secured to a bracket and hung on the wall opposite a large sideboard which was currently being filled with polished glasses. A large trestle table at the opposite end was being assembled by three girls with another waiting to lay a pristine white table cloth. And in the corner several students were blowing up white balloons with the number 10, in gold, emblazoned across the front. *Now,* thought Lilly, *where is Monica?* Due to the photographs from her on-line profile, Lilly knew what the girl looked like; tall, slim and very attractive with long chestnut hair. She spied her a moment later in the corner looking officious with a clip-board. As the girl with the box had told her, she was obviously the head organiser.

Lilly wandered over.

"Monica Morris?"

The girl glanced up, dark eyed and demure. "That's me. Can I help you?"

"Actually, I was wondering if you could spare me a few minutes? Is there somewhere we can talk in private?"

"Is it about the reunion?"

"No, it's something else. Not related to the university."

"Oh. Well, all right. I could do with a break, actually. Let's go outside it's quieter there."

She scribbled some additional notes, Lilly catching a glimpse of all the fine details which would make the reunion party a well-oiled success, then handed her clip-board to another girl explaining she'd be out in the garden if needed and exited through a side door at the back of the block. Lilly followed her into a lovely flower garden with several picnic tables and they sat down.

"It's really lovely out here, do the students maintain it?"

Monica nodded. "There are full-time gardeners for most of the property, but this area is looked after by volunteers from the agricultural courses mainly, although other students get involved, too. She took a small paper bag from her pocket and offered Lilly a ginger chew.

"No, thanks."

"So, how can I help? Sorry, what did you say your name was?" Monica asked.

"Lilly Tweed."

Monica eyed her curiously. "Do we know each other? I don't recognise your name?"

"No, we haven't met before, I'm..." it suddenly occurred to Lilly how odd it would look to appear out of nowhere asking personal questions. She would hardly have clout as a former agony aunt and current shop owner. So, with the recent spat with Abigail forefront in her mind, she just blurted out the first thing that came to her. "I'm a reporter. I was wondering if the name Carol Ann Hotch means anything to you?"

Monica started. "Is this some sort of joke?"

"A joke? No, not at all. I'm quite serious. You do know her, then?"

"Yes, I know Carol Ann. She's crazy."

"I'm sorry to have to tell you, but she's also dead, I'm afraid."

"Dead? Really? Oh, my god, I'm so sorry. Maybe I shouldn't have said that, but she's been harassing me. It's been pretty scary, actually. I had to call the police, eventually."

"Can you tell me what happened?"

"Look, I'm really not comfortable about being mentioned in the paper or anything. It's been really stressful and if I'm honest, my studies have been affected. It's made concentrating difficult when I've been constantly looking over my shoulder. I just want to forget about it and pass my exams." Suddenly her brown eyes widened as a memory obviously occurred to her. "Wait, was it her they found in the river?"

"Yes, it was," Lilly nodded. "How did you hear about it?"

"Some of the guys in my class were talking about a suicide or something, but they didn't know who it was. I wasn't really listening, just caught a few snippets, but it's not exactly a common occurrence round here, is it? I literally just put two and two together as you were speaking."

"Monica, while I was doing some research I found out, obviously correctly, you may have known Carol Ann, it's the reason I'm here. I'm hoping to learn more about her. If you don't mind me asking, how did the two of you meet?"

Monica sighed heavily and gazed off into the distance. Lilly wondered if she was going to change her mind about talking to her. Fortunately, she finally shrugged and turned back.

"I met her about a year ago at a reunion, here. Her husband was a former student, and she came with him. We hardly spoke at all during the event, but I must have made some sort of impression because she was fixated with me after that. Since then, I've been getting some crazy calls from her. Then last week..." Monica paused, seemingly reluctant to carry on.

"What happened last week?" Lilly urged gently.

"God, I hope what happened wasn't the reason she died. Did she really kill herself?"

"We don't know that for sure as yet. It could just as easily have been a tragic accident. Go on, Monica. Tell me what happened."

"She broke in here, smashed a window in the middle of the night and started screaming and shouting. She was completely hysterical. It woke everyone up. We called security and they escorted her off the premises. We didn't press charges or anything. I mean, it was obvious she wasn't in her right mind, but I messaged her husband and told him what had happened. I did say if she did it again, we'd make it official with the police and get a restraining order. I feel really awful about that now."

"What day was this?"

"A couple of days before she was found. Look, I know you'll be writing an article, but I don't want to be in the paper, okay? If she killed herself because of me then... well, you know what gossip's like, I'll get blamed even though it's not my fault."

"Don't worry, I'll keep your name out of it," Lilly assured her. "But I'd like to have a chat with some of the other girls. Maybe one of them would be willing to give me a quote instead?"

"Yes, maybe."

"Just one other thing. Do you know why Carol Ann was so fixated with you?"

"Seriously, I have absolutely no idea. Maybe I reminded her of someone else? That's the only thing I can think of because I didn't know her."

Lilly nodded. "Okay, thanks for your time, Monica. I'll let you get back."

❧

*L*ILLY SAT IN the garden for a moment after Monica had gone back inside collecting her thoughts. It seemed likely that Carol Ann had seen something in the girl that wasn't really there. Something traumatic from her past, perhaps, that had been brought to the fore on meeting Monica. A mannerism, a look, or the way she talked that reminded her of something or someone else. Lilly was pleased she'd managed to find the right Monica, but it was obviously a dead end. She got up and decided to walk through the gardens, which enveloped the building on three sides.

There were large swathes of lawn, some rising to form small hillocks where Lilly could imagine students gathering in the summer months to socialise or study. Large trees would give much needed shade on hotter days and the flower beds, where new shoots were just poking through, would be a riot of colour and scent. It was a lovely space, very calm and relaxing.

She continued to walk the pathway around the block and came across a boarded-up window at the side of the building. No doubt the one Monica had referred to. On impulse, she tried the nearby door and found it unlocked. It led directly into a large kitchen where several students were preparing food.

"Hello," said one of the girls. "Are you lost? This is for students only you really shouldn't be here."

Lilly saw another girl pick up a rolling pin, ready to swing if it became necessary. Obviously the break-in had left them nervous and wary of strangers. Understandable, she thought.

She held up her hands placatingly, "Don't worry. Reporter. I'm investigating the break-in last week. Were any of you here at the time?"

"I was," the girl with the rolling pin said. "I'm Tracey Scott."

"Do you mind if I ask you a few questions, Tracey?"

"So long as you don't mind me rolling the pastry while we talk. I've already ruined one batch of quiches."

"You're baking for the reunion, I take it?"

"That's right. We're all studying catering and hospitality. These events go towards our degree qualifications."

"So, the woman who broke in, Carol Ann, had she ever done anything like this before?"

"She's never broken in before. But that's where she got in if you're interested," Tracey said, pointing to the boarded-up window. "It was pretty frightening, I can tell you. It was the middle of the night and sounded really loud. She threw a brick through it and then climbed in. By the time we all got down here she was just standing here screaming and crying. Hands and knees covered in blood where she'd cut herself on the glass. I called security and another girl, Olivia, tried to calm her down and made her sit at the table before she hurt herself further. Or one of us. She was rambling a lot and shouting. It was a total nightmare."

"What was she rambling about?"

"Monica, she's one of the students who lives here."

"Yes, I've just been talking to her outside, actually."

"Right. Well, this woman was accusing Monica of stealing from her. Monica didn't know what she was talking about, but her presence was making Carol Ann worse. Really agitated, so we told her it would be better if she left. She waited in the common room until security came and took Carol Ann away."

Lilly glanced round the rest of the girls who were all doing other chores but listening closely. Once Tracey had finished, one of them spoke up.

"It was the first time she broke in, but it wasn't the first weird thing she did. She's shown up here before, walking around looking for Monica. We've told her she shouldn't be here, but that just made her angry. She would wait outside Monica's classes and follow her back here. About a month ago we reported it to the university security, and they started keeping an eye out for her. All visitors are supposed to sign in at reception, but it's hardly ever enforced. And it's closed at night, anyway. I think things have improved a bit since Carol Ann broke in though."

Lilly shook her head. "I didn't realise how serious it was."

"Well, breaking in was the most serious," Tracey said. "Before that, she'd just sent letters here and walked around the grounds. I think she called Monica a few times too, and she was getting really stressed about it, so we made sure she wasn't left on her own. I don't get why Carol Ann had it in for Monica, she didn't even know her. She's obviously got a bit of a screw loose. I feel a bit sorry for her if I'm honest, but it was really disturbing for all of us, especially Monica."

"Yes, I can imagine. Well, I think that's all I need. Thanks for your time. Good luck with the event."

Lilly exited the same way she had entered and paused outside the broken window. It was quite high up and glancing below she realised Carol Ann must have rolled the heavy rock in place to give herself an added boost. *She really had been determined to get in*, Lilly thought as she tried to lift the rock herself. In doing so, her pulse quickened when she saw a glint of metal. Scratching away the earth, she revealed a ring with two keys attached. On the disk were the engraved initials C.A.H.

"Carol Ann Hotch," Lilly said softly, shoving them in her pocket.

Should she try to find out what they unlocked?

*A*S LILLY WALKED back to her car, a quick glance at her phone made her realise just how late it was getting. She'd spent much longer at the university than planned and hadn't intended to leave Stacey at the shop on her own for so long. She hopped in her car and the radio came on as she started the engine. A traffic report announcing that due to an accident, the road she would normally take back to town was closed.

Of course it is, she thought. She'd better phone the shop.

"The Tea Emporium, Stacey speaking."

"Stacey, it's Lilly. I'm heading back now, but there's been a traffic accident on the main road into town so I'll have to take the scenic route. Can you manage for a while longer?"

"Yep, no problem."

"Okay, I'll be back as soon as I can."

"No need to rush. We don't want you getting in accident as well."

"My car doesn't go that fast, to be honest. See you soon."

As she pulled out of the car-park, her thoughts turned to the keys she had found. There was no doubt they belonged to Carol Ann. They were her initials and found under the rock which she'd used to boost herself through the university window. But what would they open? One was a standard Yale door key, so a house or a flat somewhere most likely. The other was much smaller, more solid and old fashioned. She had no idea what that could access. She was relieved to have found them first, though. Just as she'd been leaving, she'd heard the unmistakable voice of Abigail coming from the kitchen. However, Tracey and the other girls were in no mood to repeat themselves and flatly refused to talk to her. By now Abigail would have realised that Lilly had beaten her to it, and knowing her would be incandescent with rage. She full expected the woman to seek her out and give her a mouthful. Oh well, there was nothing she could do about it now. Her main concern was whether to hand in the keys or use them to further her investigation. It was a matter of ethics, and Lilly wasn't altogether comfortable with the way her brain was thinking.

Chapter Six

TEN MINUTES LATER, as she turned onto a long and straight stretch of road on the outskirts of town, a fancy car whipped around her right side, overtaking at a dangerous speed and in front of on-coming traffic.

"Idiot. No wonder there are so many accidents," Lilly said out loud to the reckless motorist.

She tapped the foot on the brakes to avoid getting too close as the errant driver tried to overtake another car, only to be met with a truck coming the other way. They swerved back in too close to the car in front and instinctively slammed on the brakes to avoid a collision. But Lilly didn't realise the brakes had been depressed as there were no red lights. She immediately slammed on her own, but it was too late. She clipped the bumper, causing it to spin ninety degrees and come to rest sideways across the lane. The driver's side window facing her.

"You've got to be kidding," Lilly exclaimed as she came eye to eye with a furious Abigail Douglas.

She'd never in all her years of driving been involved in an accident, and it took a short while to calm down and stop shaking before she had the presence of mind to turn on her hazard warning lights. The car which Abigail had tried to overtake had also stopped, and the driver had got out. Waiting by the passenger side of his vehicle, his warning lights flashing to alert other motorists from both directions there was an immediate hazard and to slow down. He'd be a good witness, Lilly thought as she took a deep breath and opened her door.

Abigail was already at the back of her Porsche, assessing the damage. "My car! You've hit my car. You did that deliberately, Lillian Tweed! I'm calling the police."

"Honestly, Abigail, I didn't even know it was you. Are you all right?"

"No, of course I'm not all right. Look at my car! What were you thinking?"

"Calm down and stop shouting at me. It was you who was driving like a maniac," Lilly said.

She went to the rear of the vehicle and saw the bend in the back bumper. It would need fixing, but it was hardly catastrophic. By the same token, her own car, apart from some missing paintwork, was miraculously unscathed. They had both been very lucky.

"Is that the police? Yes, I'd like to report an accident on the university road going into Plumpton Mallet. Yes, that's the one. This stupid, idiot driver just drove into the back of me and damaged my car," shrieked Abigail into her phone.

Lilly rolled her eyes. If Abigail was going to be so melodramatic, she'd be better waiting in her car for the police. She began to walk that way when she heard Abigail screech behind her.

"She's trying to leave! Wait, let me get her number plate," she shouted, running behind Lilly's car.

"I'm not trying to leave, Abigail. Don't be so ridiculous. I'm going to wait in my car so I don't have to listen to you shrieking like a banshee. And you hardly need to take note of my number plate details when you know who I am."

Back in her car, Lilly wound down her window slightly so she could still hear what Abigail was saying, and rubbed her neck. It was aching a bit. No doubt she had a bit of whiplash from the collision.

Abigail was now on another call. "Yes, of course, *that* Lillian Tweed. How many Lillian Tweeds are there in Plumpton Mallet?" she snarled. "So, I'll be late back to the office..."

Lilly picked up her own phone and sent a quick text to Stacey saying she'd been delayed. No point telling her truth and worrying her. Then she sat back and waited for the police to arrive. Ten minutes after Abigail had called, a police car pulled up behind Lilly's Mini and a familiar face got out. Sergeant Bonnie Phillips. She was Archie Brown's contact at the station and Lilly's friend. She also had a colleague with her, a younger officer who, after speaking with Bonnie, went to get a statement from the driver of the third vehicle who was still patiently waiting a few metres up the road.

"So, would you like to tell me what happened?" Bonnie asked Lilly. But before she could draw breath, Abigail interrupted.

"She drove into the back of my car. Look at the damage! I want her arrested."

"It's, Ms Douglas, isn't it? Abigail? Well, I was speaking to Miss Tweed, here. I'll get to you in a moment."

"It's all right, Bonnie. Take her statement first. I'll wait."

Lilly leant against the bonnet of her car while Bonnie took Abigail's statement. After several *'it was her fault's'* Lilly tuned out. She came back to the present as the police officer told Abigail to start her car, turn on her lights and depress the brakes.

From the rear of the Porsche, Bonnie confirmed the brake lights were out.

"With limited damage to your vehicle, I suspect these were faulty at the time, causing Miss Tweed to hit your car. Is that correct, Lilly?"

"Yes. I had no idea she had braked until it was too late."

"What rubbish," Abigail hissed. "I've only had this car a few weeks there can't be a fault such as you suggest."

"Are you calling an officer of the law a liar, Ms Douglas?"

Abigail spluttered, realising the trouble she was getting herself into, and backtracked a little. "Well no, of course not but..."

"I will be writing you a vehicle defect rectification notice for your faulty lights. I suggest you take the car to Dan's garage immediately and get them fixed. Ah, one moment, my colleague is beckoning."

Lilly watched Bonnie walk up the road, fully aware in her peripheral vision that Abigail was shooting daggers at her, but she refused to meet her gaze. After a brief conversation with her colleague and the witness, both police officers returned and the other driver left.

"Ms Douglas, having spoken to the witness and received his sworn statement, it is apparent you were driving erratically. You will shortly receive a summons to court to answer to the charge of careless driving."

"What?" Abigail staggered back, all colour draining from her face.

"Abigail," said Lilly, stepping forward. "For goodness' sake apologise. If this gets as far as court, you could lose your license. If that happens, then you could lose your job as well."

Abigail stared at Lilly as though she didn't understand what she was saying. Lilly turned to Bonnie.

"Bonnie, is this Abigail's first offence?"

Bonnie checked the police national computer from her tablet, "Yes, it is."

"Would you be prepared to let her off with a warning? There's been no one hurt, thankfully. She'll take the car to be fixed immediately she leaves here. Your colleague can even drive her car himself straight to Dan's garage. And she'll promise never to do it again. That's right, isn't it, Abigail?"

"Yes, that's right," she said, finally coming to her senses. "I apologise, officer, I was in a rush to get to the office to file my article before the deadline and wasn't thinking properly. It won't happen again."

Lilly looked at Bonnie, waiting for her response.

"You're lucky to have such an understanding friend, Ms Douglas, that's all I can say." Bonnie said eventually, much to Lilly's relief. "I suggest you take your car to be fixed now. You'll have fourteen days to provide proof to us that your lights are in full working order. You're free to go but consider this a warning. If I find out you've gone over the speed limit by as little as one mile per hour, I'll throw you in the nearest cell. Understood?"

"Yes. Yes, of course. Thank you, officer." Abigail stammered and hurriedly got in her car.

They watched her drive away, and then Bonnie turned to Lilly. "You're far too nice for your own good, you know."

Lilly shrugged. "I fully admit she is a pain in the rear end, but I don't want her to lose her job, Bonnie. Yes, she's conceited and thinks a lot of herself, but sometimes that means there's an underlying feeling of inferiority. It's possible her brash and boastful personality is a result of something in her past. Apart from her taking over my job at the paper, I don't know anything about her. Who knows what's happened in her life?"

"You're giving her the benefit of the doubt, you mean?"

Lilly nodded.

"All right, I'll accept that knowing you like I do, but remember you can't take everyone's problems on your own shoulders, Lilly. You're under no obligation to help the likes of Abigail Douglas, she, and people like her, need to be responsible for their own actions and accept the consequences accordingly."

"I know. It's a fault of mine. I'm working on it. So, how are things with you? I've not seen you since I left the paper.

I'd thought you'd have popped into the shop for a cuppa before now?"

"I thought so too, but we're a bit short staffed so I've more on my plate than usual. What with that, studying for my detective exams and now this body being found, I've hardly had time to breathe. Archie said he told you about Carol Ann Hotch when we found your letter in her pocket?"

"Yes, he did. That's why I've been out today. I found a connection between her and the university."

"The break-in at G-block, you mean? Yes, a colleague was on call for that. It's not the first incident involving Carol Ann, though."

"Oh? Anything you can share with me?"

"She called us out on her landlord a few times. Accused him of breaking into her flat in the early hours."

"Was there any truth to it?"

Bonnie shook her head. "None that we could tell. It's difficult when all you've got is a *'he-said-she-said'* dynamic. There was no sign of forced entry and what with Carol Ann's medical history, it was difficult to believe what she was saying was true."

"That's really disheartening, Bonnie."

Bonnie nodded. "So, why exactly are you getting involved with this death? It was either a tragic accident or suicide, as far as we can tell so far."

"Look, don't take this the wrong way, I'm not telling you how to do your job. But I don't think it was either. There are some things that don't add up. It's just a..."

"No, please don't say it, Lilly," Bonnie groaned.

"A gut feeling."

"You know, gut feelings and hunches are for books and television? It doesn't happen in real life. In real life we follow the evidence."

"I did say don't take it the wrong way. Apparently, Abigail Douglas thinks the same as me."

"I've known you long enough not to take it the wrong way, Lilly. I hope you'll take what I'm about to say in the same vein: Remember which one of us is the police officer."

(decorative divider)

LILLY LEFT BONNIE a few minutes later, with the police officer promising that if she heard anything that would shed new light on Carol Ann's death then she would let either Lilly or Archie know. But anything Lilly was told was not to be used as an excuse to go dashing about investigating. She might like her afternoon tea and tisanes, but she was neither Marple nor Poirot and shouldn't forget it.

She drove directly back to the shop rather than picking up her bike from home. She'd already been away much longer than intended and felt bad that she'd left Stacey to run things on her own. She parked up beside Stacey's broken-down car and dashed in the back entrance, going through the storeroom to the main shop.

Inside, Stacey was efficiently floating from customer to customer, dispensing advice on various teas and brewing samples. She rang up sales from several customers while Lilly grabbed her own apron and joined her behind the counter.

Eventually, with the shop almost empty, Lilly apologised for taking so long.

"No problem," Stacey said. "I've managed. So what happened?"

"I got into a car accident. I'm fine and so is my car, so don't worry."

"Oh, wow. I'm sorry. I won't ever joke about that again."

"I doubt you hold that much power in the cosmos, Stacey," Lilly laughed. "Anyway, while I remember, here are the details of a garage who can mend your car. Dan's an old friend, so he'll either tow it home for you or take it back and fix it, whichever you want. But if you mention my name and the fact you're a student, he'll give you a discount."

"That's cool, thanks so much. I was wondering what I was going to do about it. I'll give him a call now."

Despite the accident and being away from her business for so long, Lilly felt she'd accomplished quite a lot. She'd certainly learned a lot more about Carol Ann Hotch and also had the keys she'd found currently burning a hole in her pocket. Should she use them or give them to the police? She'd had plenty of opportunity to hand them over to Bonnie earlier, so why hadn't she? Perhaps because Bonnie was convinced there was nothing suspicious about the death? It was a dilemma and one she'd need to think about seriously. Hopefully by the time it came to closing, she'd have made her mind up about how to proceed.

*B*ACK AT HOME she fed Earl then heated up some lasagna for herself. Taking her plate and cup to the table, she turned on her laptop and with Carol Ann's letter by her side, made a search for her address. It didn't take her long to find the building. A former bijou hotel owned by a single landlord had been converted into eight flats. As many of the larger properties on the periphery of the town had been, sadly. They obviously were no longer financially viable as single resident dwellings.

It wasn't a part of the town she'd had much reason to visit previously, being at the opposite end to both her home and her shop, but she knew vaguely where it was. She quickly snapped a picture on her phone, then took her empty plate to the sink.

"So what do you think, Earl? Bonnie's right, I'm not a police officer, but there's something niggling at me about this case. I mean, Carol Ann wrote to me asking for help. I have her keys in my pocket. What harm could it do just to check her flat and see if there's something inside that would help determine what happened to her one way or another?"

Earl jumped onto the counter and giving a loud meow, head-butted her arm. She reached out and scratched his ears, feeling the immediate purr reverberating beneath her fingers.

"Yes, you're right. I've already made my mind up, haven't I?"

A few minutes later Lilly had changed into jeans and a warm jumper. She grabbed her fleece from the hook in the hall and shouting goodbye to Earl, locked up and grabbed her bike. If the on-line map was correct, there was a short-cut she could use which would avoid the main roads and end up not far from Carol Ann's home.

She turned left outside her garden gate and rode to the top of the lane, then took another left to join the pathways that ran alongside the river. Ten minutes later, she turned right onto a cycle trail that ran through the woods. It was still light enough to see even with the overhead canopy of Evergreens, but her return journey would have to take another route. Obviously there was no light source through the woods and it would be foolhardy and dangerous to attempt to cycle through it in the dark, and it would be too far to walk even if she could see where she was going. She cycled for a further fifteen minutes, then not far from the exit and close to the road where Carol Ann's building was, she was forced to stop when her phone rang. It was Archie. She dismounted and continued on foot, pushing the bike to her destination while they talked.

"I don't know how you did it, Lilly, but your instincts were bang on."

"In what way?"

"I've just got word from Abigail. The wretched woman muscled in on my investigation again by answering my phone and pretending we were working together. Can you believe her cheek? Anyway, at least she had the decency to share what she'd found out. It was the autopsy results on Carol Ann. She overdosed."

"Ah, okay. That's really sad news to hear, Archie. But why does that mean my instincts were correct? My thoughts were the opposite. I didn't think it was suicide, but if it was an overdose after all..."

"Well, that's the thing," Archie said, his excitement at genuine news palpable. "There were abrasions inside her mouth and some other indicators that she wasn't alone. Bruising, etc. I can't give you all the official medical terminology. But, to cut a long story short, Lilly, someone forced the tablets down her throat. You were right all along. The police are now treating it as murder."

⊗⊗⊗⊗⊗

"I KNEW IT!" LILLY exclaimed. "There was something about this whole scenario that just didn't feel right. Oh, poor Carol Ann... I can't begin to imagine what she went through. She must have been terrified."

"So, tell me, what do you actually know? I just got an earful from Abigail when she got back to the office. Did you really crash into her car?"

"Oh, for heaven's sake. What's she been saying?"

"That you both got into an accident coming back from St. John's. She suggested you may have done it deliberately."

"Well, quite frankly that's a lie, Archie. She was driving like a lunatic and her brake lights didn't work. She made an emergency stop having tried and failed to overtake the car in front with traffic coming the other way, and I ran into the back of her. It was a complete accident and one I had no hope of avoiding. I don't suppose she told you that Bonnie was about to arrest her for dangerous driving, which would have meant she could have lost her license, her job and possibly gone to prison?"

"No, it must have slipped her mind to share that nugget of information. So Bonnie attended the scene did she?"

"Yes. And it was only the fact that I persuaded her to let Abigail off with a ticket and caution that she was allowed to go at all."

Archie barked out a laugh. "You are much too nice, Lilly Tweed."

"Bonnie said the same thing. I'm beginning to think you're right now you've told me Abigail is blaming me. A charming way to repay a favour isn't it? I hope no one believes her."

"Don't worry, they don't. We've got the measure of Abigail Douglas. But I'm curious what you two were doing at the university in the first place?"

"I went there trying to track down someone Carol Ann may have known," Lilly explained. "I subsequently found out she broke into student accommodation; G-Block and caused a scene. I think Abigail had uncovered details of the break-in and had gone to ask about that."

"But you went to talk to someone specific? Who?" Archie asked. "Give me a leg up on Abigail, would you? She's really starting to annoy me the way she's barging in on my job. I'm running several investigations at once, while she's only got this case, so she's beating me to the punch on this one every time. She's making me look incompetent."

"I don't mind helping you, Archie, but you must give me your word that you won't let this girl know you got her name from me? And more importantly, that her name won't appear in the paper? She made me promise her, and she's been through a lot already with Carol Ann. She's already falling behind on her course work due to the stress, and I think she's pretty close to breaking point. For some reason Carol Ann was utterly obsessed with her."

"Cross my heart, Lilly. And a good newspaperman never reveals his sources."

"Okay, her name is Monica Morris."

"Thanks, Lilly."

"Excuse me, can I help you?" a voice said. Lilly had arrived at Carol Ann's home a minute or two previously and had been leaning on the palings surrounding the communal garden at the front while chatting with Archie. She turned and came face-to-face with a stocky, florid looking man with a stern frown.

"Archie, I've got to go. Let me know if anything interesting turns up."

"Likewise. Bye for now, Lilly."

She hung up and warily faced the man in front of her, sincerely hoping there wouldn't be any trouble.

Chapter Seven

"HELLO, DO YOU live here?" Lilly began.

"Why, are you looking for a flat?"

"Sort of. I'm looking for Carol Ann Hotch's place?"

The man's frown deepened. "What business do you have with Carol Ann?" he asked sharply.

"She recently passed away..." Lilly began, but the man interrupted her.

"Yes, I know. The police informed me this morning. I'm Barney Darwin. I own the building. Are you with the police?"

"No, nothing like that. My name is Lillian Tweed, Carol Ann wrote to me shortly before she died."

"You're the agony aunt for the paper?" he said.

Lilly nodded. "I used to be."

"Yeah, I thought I recognised the name. I wrote to you once. Long time ago now. Anonymously, but you helped me out. It was great advice, actually."

"I'm glad I could help you."

"So, what are you doing here, Miss Tweed?"

"Well, as I was saying, I received a letter from Carol Ann shortly before she was found in the river. She was asking for my help, but she died before we could meet. I'm trying to get some answers, I suppose. I understand from a police sergeant friend that she gave her landlord some trouble in the past. That would be you, would it?"

Barney sighed heavily and stuck both hands in his jacket pockets. "She was a nice woman, but she had some problems. Paranoia, seeing things that weren't there, that sort of thing. She was a little crazy, to be honest. I expect you know all about that? She called the police on me two, maybe three times accusing me of breaking into her flat. Which was ridiculous. I don't have any business being in one of my tenant's homes unless they need something fixing. And then I make an appointment."

"What made her think you were breaking in?"

"Miss Tweed, if I knew, I'd tell you. Sometimes I'd see her in her garden at the back and she'd randomly shout about how she'd seen me in her kitchen during the night. No truth to it, but she believed what she was saying because she was ill, so I couldn't really blame her. She had hallucinations apparently, normal for the problem she had, where she would see or hear things that didn't exist outside her own mind. I put it down to that."

"It must have been a nuisance for you?"

He shrugged. "Yeah, but the police were pretty understanding after it happened the first time. It got on my nerves a bit, sure. You never know what other people might think, do you? Even though it wasn't true it could easily have ruined my reputation. You know how the saying goes, no smoke without fire? But in this case, there was. Luckily folk realised it was all in her mind and she couldn't help it. It was her illness. She once told me she thought the paperboy was a government spy, I mean how ridiculous does that sound? But she was unstable, especially if she forgot to take her tablets. I was always sorry I couldn't do more to help her, but she was suffering from paranoid delusions."

Not that paranoid, Lilly thought. *Someone did kill her.*

"I was hoping you'd let me into her flat," she said, cutting to the chase.

Barney was visibly surprised at the question. "What? No, of course I won't, it's private property. Besides, her husband is coming along shortly to start clearing the place out."

Lilly nodded. "Yes, of course, I understand. I was just looking for answers, that's all."

"Well, you won't find them here, Miss Tweed. I suggest you go home and leave things to the police."

"I suppose you're right," Lilly said with a smile. "Thanks for your time, Mr Darwin."

She gripped the bike's handlebars and began to wheel it away from the railings, up the road. Out of the corner of her eye, she watched as the landlord approached and entered the front ground-floor flat.

He obviously hadn't realised it, but he'd given Lilly a clue as to which flat had belonged to Carol Ann. The large

Victorian building had been broken up into eight flats; four on the ground floor, two at the front and two at the back, mirrored on the second floor. The front ground floor flats shared the communal gardens, but the ones on the ground floor at the rear had their own. There were only two of them, and Barney had mentioned seeing Carol Ann in her garden. Lilly only had to try the key in two locks to find the one she wanted.

She wheeled her bike around the side of the building and leant it up against the wall. Creeping to the edge, she peered around the corner and discovered high fencing surrounding the plots. At the end there were two tall wood gates, one for each flat. The first flat had a light on, which made Lilly's job much easier.

She carefully opened the gate of the second garden and tip toed down the path to the door. The flat, as expected, was in total darkness. Taking the Yale key, she inserted it into the lock. It turned with a satisfying click. She was in.

*F*OR OBVIOUS REASONS she didn't dare turn on any of the lights, but there was a torch function on her phone which would work well. She had entered straight into a small galley kitchen. She shone the torch around briefly, but there was nothing much to see. No cups or plates in the sink, nothing on the worktops except a white microwave, a silver kettle and matching toaster. The cupboards revealed the usual things a kitchen would house, but there was nothing that would help her.

She moved across the central hall into the room opposite, a lounge with a window looking onto the garden, framed in faded green and blue chintz curtains. Again the place was pristine, almost austere. One double seat sofa and a matching armchair in grey cord. A nest of small tables and a plain blue rug in front of a gas fire. On the chimney breast was an old art deco style mirror hanging from a picture hook by a chain. There were no knick-knacks or photos. No books or magazines. Nothing personal at all. It was the least homely home Lilly had ever been in, and she wondered how long Carol Ann had actually been living here?

She returned to the small hall and found the bathroom, again almost empty. A couple of green towels hanging over the bath and a bottle of shampoo in the corner. A bar of soap, a toothbrush and a toothpaste tube on the sink. The mirror faced cupboard above was completely empty. No sign it had ever been used at all, which Lilly found odd. Finally she entered the last room at the rear, which was the bedroom. Even here it was apparent Carol Ann had not really settled in. There was a single photograph in a silver frame on her nightstand, a picture of her in happier days with a handsome, dark haired man who she assumed was her husband.

The wardrobe revealed a neat but sparse row of clothing. Lilly diligently went through the pockets but came up empty handed. Shining the torch on the floor of the wardrobe, she found something far more interesting. A small steel safe. Crouching down, she examined it further. Pulling to the side a little metal disk revealed a key hole. One that would take a small, old-fashioned key. Lilly smiled and brought out the keys she'd found at St. John's. As she'd hoped, the small one unlocked the safe.

Inside, she found an antique pocket watch and a single photograph. She closed the safe and took the items to the bed where she could get a better look. Shining the torch on the photo, she was shocked to discover it was of none other than Monica Morris, smiling happily with a small white dog in her arms. A Pomeranian.

"I've seen something like this before. I know I have. But where?" Lilly muttered. Then she remembered. She grabbed her phone and began hurriedly scrolling through the images until she found the one she wanted. It was the photo Archie had given her of Carol Ann Hotch. The one where she was holding a small, white Pomeranian dog.

"No wonder Carol Ann was so obsessed with her. All that following her around and accusing her of being a thief. Monica must have stolen her dog."

Suddenly she caught a familiar noise. One she really didn't want to hear. Someone had just unlocked the front door and entered the flat. She hurriedly stuffed the photograph and the watch in her pocket and dashed to the bedroom door. Peering out, she saw a man crossing the hallway from the kitchen to the lounge. Heart pounding, Lilly stepped back into the bedroom, intent on finding a way to escape. Too late she realised there wasn't a window. She was trapped.

*L*ILLY TOOK A deep breath. Breaking and entering 101; be confident and pretend you belong there. She'd read that somewhere. It was probably nonsense, but what did she have to lose?

The light turned on and the man jumped back in shock, bumping into the hall wall.

"Hey! Who are you? What are you doing in my wife's flat?"

"Mr Hotch? I am so sorry, I didn't know you were coming. I'm Lilly Tweed, your wife wrote to me just before she died. Please accept my condolences for your loss."

There was a moment's pause as he considered her words. "All right. But that still doesn't explain what you're doing in here. How did you get in?"

"The door was unlocked." Admittedly she shouldn't have lied, but it was instinctual. Besides, there was no going back now. "I shouldn't have come in, I know, but..."

"No, you shouldn't. I've come to collect her belongings, but you still haven't told me what you're doing here?"

"Your wife wrote to me, like I said. I used to be the agony aunt with the Gazette. In her letter she sounded terribly distressed and I wrote back asking to meet so I could help. Apparently my letter was found in her pocket when she was pulled from the river. I've been distraught about the whole thing and was just looking for answers about what happened. I thought there might be something here that could help me. It's for my own peace of mind, really. I just wish I'd been able to help her."

Joseph's expression softened slightly. Now she looked at him closely he looked exhausted and grief-stricken.

"Believe me, Miss Tweed, you're not the only one. I shouldn't have let her move here. I knew she shouldn't have been alone for an extended length of time. That she wouldn't cope. But she was so insistent, and my attempts at trying to dissuade her just made things worse. I should have come and got her sooner."

"Why was she here, if you don't mind me asking?"

There was a momentary tension in his jaw as he gritted his teeth. Lilly was afraid she'd intruded too much, but then he relaxed again and replied.

"We were separated. For about a year now. She's been fighting a losing battle with schizophrenia for a long time and her paranoia was gaining ground. If I'm being honest, I was growing frustrated with it all. I needed a break, so when she packed up and told me she was leaving, I eventually gave in and let her go. I should have made a better effort to stop her, I knew if she left home she'd forget to take a medication, but I was thinking of myself. It was selfish and now I'll have to live with the guilt of knowing she would still have been alive if only..."

Lilly could see the pain and guilt etched in the man's face. Mental illness was incredibly difficult for a partner to deal with, and Joseph Hotch had obviously been living with it for a long time. Watching his wife spiralling out of control must have been heartbreaking. It was hardly surprising he wanted a break from it all.

"I know it sounds a bit hackneyed, but you can't blame yourself. Someone is responsible for taking Carol Ann's life. That's the person you should blame."

"You know the police think it's murder now, then?"

Lilly nodded. "I have a friend at the station."

"It made more sense to me when they told me it was suicide. I don't know what to think now."

"Do you know anyone who would want to harm your wife, Mr Hotch?"

"No one at all. She was a bit of a nuisance when the demons took over, but I can't imagine anyone wanting to kill her. She had such a good heart and always meant well when she was taking her medication. I can't understand why anyone would want to hurt her. Surely Carol Ann should have evoked sympathy and compassion? Even at her worst, she wasn't a threat."

"Unfortunately, people are often fearful of things they don't understand."

Joseph nodded. "I suppose so. Look, I need to get on now, I appreciate you listening, and your kind wish to help my wife, but you really have no business being here. And this is a job I would prefer to do on my own."

"Of course, I'll get out of your way."

She left the bedroom and returned down the hall to the kitchen. Joseph Hotch followed her. At the back door she hesitated a moment, wondering if she should ask a final question. Carol Ann's letter had mentioned her husband, but this was a tricky situation. The man was in mourning for a murdered wife. But at the same time, he was also a suspect. She didn't know him, so how volatile was he? What should she do? It was Joseph himself that made up her mind.

"Is there something else, Miss Tweed?"

Lilly opened the back door and stepped into the garden before turning back. She needed the security of being able to run should it be necessary. She took a deep breath and spoke.

"ACTUALLY, YES, THERE is one more thing and believe me when I say I'm really sorry to have to ask it, but in your wife's letter to me she mentioned an affair. Were you cheating on her, Mr Hotch?"

Lilly had never witnessed a person's complexion go from sallow to puce in the blink of an eye. Clearly this was one question too far. She retreated up the garden path as Joseph Hotch took a threatening step forward and yelled at her.

"How dare you! Get out before I have you arrested and don't come back."

"I'm sorry," Lilly stammered just as the door slammed shut.

She could feel the adrenaline pumping through her body as she bolted round the side of the building back to her bike. She wanted to put as much distance between herself and Joseph Hotch as possible. She shook her head, disappointed in herself as she mounted her bike and set off home. She could have, *should have*, handled it much better. She'd already irritated him enough simply by being in his wife's flat in the first place, but he'd been gracious enough to answer her questions. He was grieving, and now she felt awful for pushing him to that level of anger. Her timing really had been terrible, she'd added another layer of unnecessary anguish when he was already going through the most dreadful difficulties. However, Joseph Hotch was still a suspect. In fact, he was the prime one. Lilly knew the police would always look to family members first before widening their search. Could Carol Ann's disease have pushed him over the edge? Made him angry and bitter at what he saw as his wasted life, caring for someone who was so ill that a chance of a normal, loving relationship was never going to happen? Enough to want to free himself from the burden without divorce or the associated public shame of abandoning a sick wife?

As she road home the long way, she also realised Joseph Hotch hadn't answered her question. Carol Ann was sure her husband had been having an affair, but did her accusation have any merit considering her mental health issues? Perhaps she had confronted him and he'd killed her in order to keep her quiet? If so, who was the other woman? Could the mystery woman be the guilty party? It was just another layer of confusion for Lilly to try to peel back, and her head was spinning.

Perhaps Joseph Hotch was exactly what he appeared to be, a mourning husband who had done all he could to take care of and protect a very sick wife. He had been wracked with guilt when he'd admitted to his desire for a break, yet had stayed with her for years trying to help. It was a level of dedication Lilly couldn't help but admire.

Her mind then turned to Carol Ann's landlord, Barney Darwin. Everything he had said sounded perfectly plausible. But what if he was lying? Bonnie had said there was no proof he had broken in. It was his word against Carol Ann's. But on the other hand, there was nothing to say he hadn't either.

Were her delusions the reason Carol Ann had been a perfect target? Had Barney taken advantage of the fact no one would believe her when he was accused? Her flat had looked to Lilly as though it had never been a home. There were no personal items that would make it such. Maybe Barney had been letting himself in on a regular basis and taking her things to sell on, secure in the knowledge that no one would ever find out?

By the time she got home, she was mentally and physically exhausted. She was looking forward to a relaxing bath and an early night. Perhaps in the morning things would make more sense.

It wasn't until she hung up her fleece that she remembered the photograph and pocket watch she'd taken from Carol Ann's safe. She closed her eyes and rested her forehead on the wall as her stupidity took hold. She'd just stolen potential evidence in a murder inquiry.

Chapter Eight

NEXT MORNING LILLY transferred the photo and watch from her fleece jacket pocket to her bag, making a mental note to call Bonnie about them later. She decided to take the car to work. After all the cycling she'd done the previous evening, her legs ached too much to do it again today. Besides, with Stacey's car in the garage, she could give her lift home if needed. It would save her having to spend her wages on taxi fares.

Once again, she parked in the rear car-park and entered through the storeroom door. Inside the main shop she saw Stacey standing at the front door waiting to get in. She'd returned the keys to Lilly previously, but if she was going to be first to arrive, then it would make sense if she had her own set.

She let Earl out of his carrier where he promptly made a beeline for his usual spot, then opened the front door, locking it again after Stacey was inside. There were still twenty minutes to go before they opened.

"Morning, Lilly," Stacey said brightly. "I was expecting to see you on your bike like always."

"I brought the car this morning so if you need a lift home later just let me know."

"I don't mind taking a cab."

"I know you don't but you're going to have a garage bill to pay shortly and taxi rides add up. The offer's there if you want it."

Stacey grinned. "Yeah, that would be great, actually. Thanks, Lilly."

They both went straight to work getting the place ready for the day. Restocking items, checking the till float and straightening the displays. While Stacey ran a quick duster around the shelves, Lilly boiled the kettle. It had become a morning routine to brew a different pot of tea for just the two of them in a morning. She would either quiz Stacey on what she had learned, or if it was a new tea would talk her through its health benefits and history while she wrote down the details. It was a ritual they both enjoyed.

At nine-o'clock on the dot, Stacey flipped the sign to open and unlocked the door.

"I'm going to work in the shop this morning," Lilly said. "Would you be okay working on clearing and organising the back store room and the upstairs flat?"

"Sure. I love doing that stuff."

Lilly was kept busy for most of the morning with both regular customers coming in to restock or pick up orders, and much to her delight several new ones. She'd recently taken delivery of a new product line; three and four tier vintage sandwich and cake stands, perfect for afternoon tea. She'd placed one in the window that morning and already had sold all but two. She scribbled a note to order more.

At lunch time Stacey popped to their favourite bakery for sandwiches and ate in the back room first, but made Lilly promise she wouldn't peek in the storeroom. She wanted it to be a surprise. So an amused Lilly took her lunch across to a bench in the square and ate there.

A hectic afternoon followed and Stacey took time from her tidying up to help in the shop. About an hour before closing time the rain started and with the shop empty of customers Lilly was finally allowed in the back to see what had been accomplished.

Stacey stood in the door way to keep one eye on the shop while Lilly stared at the scene before her. The place was unrecognisable from the chaotic mess it had been that morning. Shelves were rearranged and stacked with merchandise, all neatly labelled, so it was easy to see at a glance what products were running low.

The small staff kitchen had been scrubbed and the table where they ate their lunch was adorned with a colourful table cloth, which Lilly recognised as being part of the upstairs flat. Stacey had even made a cosy corner for Earl with his alternative bed lifted onto a small table. Lilly knew cats preferred to be up high, it gave them a good vantage point from where they could spot any dangers. And as if to prove the point, Earl sauntered through to the back room and jumped straight in, beginning to paddle and purring loudly.

"Well, that's a first!" Lilly exclaimed. "Stacey, you have done a fantastic job, I hardly recognise the place."

"Hey, I loved doing it."

"Let me go and have a look upstairs too, then we can close up."

The upstairs was just as pristine as downstairs. All the products had been removed and were now where they should be, in the storeroom. It was a tremendous effort, and Lilly was incredibly grateful to Stacey for doing so much work. It was something she'd been putting off for a while, being too tired at the end of a working day to tackle such a big job. But now it was done, she'd make sure it stayed that way.

"Well done, Stacey. Seriously, that is a load off my mind." She said once back downstairs. "Let's close up and I'll take you home. You've earned it."

＊＊＊

"DO YOU WANT to come in for a coffee?" Stacey asked when they arrived outside her flat. Lilly smiled. "That sounds lovely. Is it okay if I bring Earl?"

"Absolutely, he's part of the family."

In the kitchen, while Stacey put the coffee pot on, Lilly let Earl out and sunk into a seat at the table. She noticed there were signs Stacey had tried to improve the place since her last visit. The peeling wallpaper had been glued, the mould spots scrubbed clean, and several sample pots of paint, in dusky pinks and greens, were sitting on a shelf.

"You've been busy here, too. I like the paint colours."

"Yeah, doing my best. The paint reminds me of home. They're my mom's favourite colours." Stacey said, handing Lilly a mug of coffee. "Not sure how much I can improve it, though. I'd rather spend my time finding a better place, but they're either out of my price range or just as bad."

"I had a thought about that, actually. You'd prefer to be in the town, I think you said?"

"Definitely, but prices in town are way out of my budget."

"What do you pay here?"

"Five hundred pounds a month, with bills on top. It's cheap compared to other places, but you get what you pay for, I guess."

"Good grief, Stacey. You are definitely paying more than this place is worth. It's a bit of health hazard to say the least. And if I'm honest, I'm not really happy with you having to live here. My plan was always to rent out the flat above the shop when it was cleared out. Which you've managed to do now. Would you be interested?"

"Wow! Yes, of course I would. But I can't afford the rates in town, even with my grant. I've trawled everywhere looking, believe me."

Lilly shrugged. "The rate is what I would say it is, I own the whole building. At the moment it's a waste of potential as it's not earning me anything. So how about you pay the same as you do here?"

"Are you serious?"

"Don't get me wrong, Stacey, it's not wholly altruistic on my part, although I really would like to see you get out of this hovel. I would benefit greatly from having the person renting the flat also working in the shop, but it would make you easily accessible if I needed additional help at any time. You'd need to consider whether or not you'd be happy living above where you work and the fact that I may call on you at a moment's notice because you'd be so near."

"Are you kidding me! I'd love it! But are you sure? I mean, I know you could rent it out for twice as much as you'd be charging me."

"Of course, I'm sure. Though in exchange, I may ask you to open up on your own some mornings? What do you say?"

Stacey jumped up, tears of joy in her eyes, and gave Lilly a fierce hug. "Thank you so much. My neighbour is a nightmare, plays music at all hours. I can't wait!" she sprang back and knocked Lilly's bag off the table, scattering the contents.

"Oh no. I'm so sorry. Got a bit excited there. Let me get everything." She passed the bag back to Lilly and on hands and knees began collecting the items. Keys, lipstick, a pen, diary and eventually the watch.

"Oh wow! I can't believe you have one of these."

"What?" Lilly asked, holding out her hand to take the pocket watch from an amazed Stacey.

"It's a Patek Philippe. My stepfather got one when he retired from the company he worked for. They're worth about eight thousand dollars on average. More if it's a special edition type. How long have you had it?"

"Eight thousand dollars?" Lilly squeaked. "Are you sure? How much is that in pounds?"

"About six thousand, I think."

"Oh no..." Lilly's stomach dropped. She'd stolen a pocket watch worth a small fortune. She was surprised the police hadn't already come knocking on her door.

"Lilly, what's wrong?"

Lilly explained everything, from being at the college and finding the keys. To entering Carol Ann's flat and discovering the safe.

"When I heard the door open and footsteps coming down the hall, I panicked and just stuffed it in my pocket before I had a chance to think. I'm such an idiot. Joseph Hotch must know Carol Ann had the watch if it's that valuable, and surely he's realised by now it's missing from the safe? His first thought is going to be that I was the one who stole it."

"Maybe he thinks she sold it or something? Besides, you've got the keys, right? There may not be another one to the safe so he can't open it."

"Actually, Stacey, that's a very good point. But I still can't risk holding on to it. I meant to call Bonnie, my police friend, about it today, but we were so busy it slipped my mind. I need to return it and own up to what I did before it all gets out of hand. I really didn't mean to keep it."

"Man, I can't believe my boss is a cat burglar!"

"Stacey!"

Suddenly they both burst into uncontrollable laughter. *The whole thing was so ridiculous you had to see the funny side,* thought Lilly.

"So, was that the only thing you pinched?"

"No, actually," Lilly said with a blush, which made Stacey giggle even more, reaching into her pocket for the photograph and handing it over.

"Wait, I think I know her. I've seen her around campus with that little dog before. I can't remember her name though. She's a year or two above me."

"Monica."

"Yeah, that's it."

"When I was at St John's the other day, some of the girls said Carol Ann thought Monica had stolen from her." She reached into her bag and brought out the photo Archie had given her. "Have a look at this."

"Oh, wow. It looks like the same dog. You think she stole the poor woman's puppy?"

"I don't know. It seems a really cruel thing to do and I can't think why she would do it. Plus, she wasn't exactly hiding it, was she? I think I'll go to the university in the morning and ask Monica about it, see what she says."

"You want me to open up?"

"No, it's all right. I'll need to drop Earl in at the shop before I go."

"Well, be careful. You don't want to get in any more trouble."

THE SUN WAS shining the next morning and while she would have preferred to bike to work, it would have to be the car today if she was to visit Monica at St John's as planned. She parked in the rear car park and grabbed Earl's carrier, entering through the store room. She was just unlocking the front shop door when Stacey appeared.

"Good morning. Great day, isn't it? So glad the sun is shining it means we should be busy."

"Let's hope so. Oh, and while I remember, I've brought the spare shop keys for you." Lilly said, handing over a key ring with a miniature floral china teapot hanging off it.

"Awesome! Thanks so much, Lilly."

"Look after them. They are the only spares I've got."

"No problem. But maybe we should see about having another set cut, just in case?"

Lilly nodded. The girl was right, and she made a mental note to get it done sometime this week.

They spent twenty minutes setting the shop up and chatting briefly over a cup of chamomile tea with honey, then it was time for Lilly to go.

"I shouldn't be too long, but if I'm delayed for any reason, I'll let you know."

Once again she parked in the same place she had previously, and where she'd had the unfortunate run in with Abigail. It had obviously disturbed her more than she'd thought as she found herself looking over her shoulder more than once. Fortunately Abigail didn't appear and Lilly, having once again signed in at reception first, made her way to G-block unmolested. On the steps at the front of the building two female students were comparing notes, text books and highlighter pens in hand.

"Hi," Lilly said. "I'm looking for Monica Morris, is she around?"

"Still in chemistry class, but she should be back soon. You're welcome to wait inside if you want?"

"I appreciate that, thanks." She made her way into the entrance hall. The place was much calmer than her previous visit, and the common room, fully set up for the reunion now, was thankfully devoid of people. Settling on a small sofa, she waited for Monica to arrive. She wasn't alone long.

"I can't believe you had the gall to come back here," a tremulous voice said a few minutes later.

Lilly stood up. "Monica..." she began. Obviously the girl had learned the truth.

"You're not a reporter, are you? Another woman turned up shortly after you left the other day, asking the same questions. We told her we'd already spoken to a reporter, but she made out she didn't know who we meant. I never mentioned your name, but I got the feeling she knew it was you, anyway. She left eventually, but I decided to look you up and found you were sacked from The Plumpton Mallet Gazette months ago. You were only the agony aunt and got replaced when the paper was bought out. So why are you even asking questions about Carol Ann Hotch?"

Lilly took a deep breath. "You're right, Monica, I shouldn't have said I was a reporter. It was a spur-of-the-moment decision so as not to alarm you and one which I now regret. But I needed to speak to you about Carol Ann. Yes, I was the paper's agony aunt for many years. I wasn't sacked but was made redundant. However, many people still write to me for help. Carol Ann was one of those people. Her letter upset me a great deal, but before I had a chance to help she was found dead. I've felt dreadful about it ever since."

Monica sighed then carelessly threw her bag then herself on the sofa. "You should have just told me."

"Yes, I know I should. Would you have still talked to me if I had done, though?"

"I don't know. Maybe. So what do you want now?"

"I've recently come across something about Carol Ann and wondered if you could help me with it?"

"You know, I am so tired of hearing that name. I just want to forget about her. I don't know anything. Really, I don't."

"Could you just look at a couple of photos for me?"

"Okay, fine."

Lilly handed over the first picture, the one of Carol Ann. "This was given to me by a friend at the paper. And this one was found in Carol Ann's flat." She handed her the second picture of herself with the dog.

"She had a picture of me?" Monica said, looking at Lilly in shock. "Why? That's really disturbing."

"Well, I think it's because of the dog you're both holding. One of your house mates said she'd been accusing you of stealing something from her. Was it her dog?"

"What? No, of course not! Why would I steal her dog? That's ridiculous. Is that what she was so upset with me about?"

"I think so." Said Lilly. "Is that not the case?"

"No, it's not even the same dog." She held up the picture of herself and pointed to the dog. "This is Pipsqueak. My dog. It took me ages to name her, but she lets out a little squeak when she's excited. It suits her. She lives with my parents most of the time as I can't keep her here." She thrust out the other photo. "The dog in this picture would be much older now and actually died about a year ago. These pictures were taken ages apart. Carol Ann was a crazy woman who missed her dog and obviously wanted mine. I can't believe this is what it's all been about."

"They look exactly the same."

"Of course. They're from the same breeder."

"So, you just happened to choose the same breeder as Carol Ann, only years apart?" Lilly asked, a slightly sceptical tone in her voice. "That's a bit of a coincidence, wouldn't you say?"

"It wasn't a coincidence at all, actually." Monica replied with strained patience. "I met her husband here, remember, at one of the reunions? Well, he's the breeder. He showed me some pictures of the puppies he had available and I fell in love with Pipsqueak and got her."

Lilly clasped her hands, staring at Monica. "You didn't tell me all this when I spoke to you. You seem to have more in common with the Hotch's than you let on."

"I hardly know them. Look," she said, counting off the points on her fingers. "I met them at the reunion. Joseph told me about the puppies. I asked to see them. He showed me photos, and I chose one. That's it."

Lilly sighed. "So, you think Carol Ann convinced herself that the puppy in your picture was her old dog that had died?"

"I have no idea. I don't even know where she got the picture. All I know is she started following me around, accusing me of stuff I didn't do and making me really uncomfortable. I tried to ignore it because it was obvious she was ill, but it got worse. The break in was the last straw, and I called security.

Look, I'm sorry, but I don't want to talk about it anymore. If you have any more questions, then I suggest you talk to her husband. I have to study."

Lilly watched as Monica got up and strode purposefully from the room. A moment later she heard footsteps running up the stairs. She leaned back, feeling deflated. She hadn't learned much more at all. The fact Joseph Hotch bred dogs could be easily proved, but how did that help in regard to Carol Ann's death? She couldn't work out a connection, and if she was honest, it hadn't moved her investigation forward in the slightest. *And I don't think I'll get anything more out of Monica,* she thought.

She was about to leave when she noticed Monica's bag beside her. The girl had been in such a rush to leave she'd forgotten it.

*L*ILLY QUICKLY GLANCED to the door to make sure she was alone, then turned back to the bag. *Don't even think about it!* Her mind warned her. But her curiosity was too strong. Gingerly, she lifted the flap. There was the usual paraphernalia associated with a student; notebook and pens alongside a study book. A pink purse was tucked in the bottom next to a packet of mints, the ginger chews the girl had offered Lilly the first time they'd met, vitamins and a lipstick. But it was the letter that made her catch her breath. A letter she had no business having.

Her mind was working overtime as she carefully withdrew it from the bag. Suddenly she heard clamouring voices and a multitude of footsteps on the stairs. Quickly, she stuffed the letter in her pocket and left the room. The students she'd met on the way in had gone, so she hurried down the steps unseen and jogged to her car. Safely inside, she took out the letter and began to read.

Carol Ann,

> *I insist you stop this ridiculous and dangerous behaviour and come home immediately. I don't know what you think has happened, but you must know it's not real. It's all in your mind. Have your therapy sessions taught you nothing? You're making a fool of yourself, not to mention embarrassing me. If you carry on the way you are, you're going to get yourself in serious trouble and I won't be able to help you then. I had another call from the university. What on earth were you doing? You must leave that poor girl alone before she has you arrested. I'm getting tired of it all, Carol Ann. For everyone's sake come home before I'm left with no other choice. I don't want to do something I'll regret.*

Joseph

It certainly wasn't a love letter, which had been Lilly's first thought. It also painted a rather different picture of Joseph Hotch from the loving, caring husband who would do anything to help his wife. Mind you, she'd seen him go from sad and dejected to furious so fast it had made her head spin. He obviously had a temper.

She folded the letter and slipped it into her bag alongside the watch and photo. "You're fast turning into a kleptomaniac, Lillian Tweed." She muttered.

She mulled over the letter and the information about the dogs Monica had given her for a while before making a decision and reaching for her phone. She should at least confirm the dog story. Scrolling through her phone contacts, she reached the letter J. If anyone could confirm it, it would be Dr Jorgenson, Carol Ann's therapist. He'd given Lilly his private number when she'd been to visit him so, providing he wasn't with a client, he should answer himself. He did.

"Miss Tweed?"

"Yes. Hello, Dr Jorgenson. I'm sorry to bother you. I wondered if you had a minute to answer a question I have about Carol Ann?"

There was a heavy and slightly exasperated sigh down the line. "Miss Tweed, as I explained before, I really can't discuss my patients with you."

"I know, but it's not about Carol Ann per se, it's about her dog."

"Her dog? You mean Scooter?"

"I don't know it's name. Was it a small white Pomeranian?"

"Yes, that's right."

"What can you tell me about it?"

"He was a gift from her husband and she adored him. They went everywhere together, and she really looked after him well. Having something else to care for made her look after herself better. Scooter was totally reliant on her you see, and she loved him. He was almost like her child, actually. He died about a year ago, I think. Hit by a car, unfortunately. It was extremely traumatic for Carol Ann, as you can imagine. It was one of the primary causes of her relapse."

"A year ago? So, that would be around the time she and Joseph separated?" Lilly asked.

There was a distinct pause. "Yes, I suppose that's correct. Is that all, Miss Tweed, I have a client due?"

"Just one more question if you don't mind. Do you know if Joseph Hotch bred Pomeranians?"

"Yes, he did, that's how Carol Ann got Scooter in the first place. Miss Tweed, what on earth is this about?"

"I'm not sure yet, Dr Jorgenson. It may mean nothing. But I appreciate your help. Bye for now."

She ended the call and sighed. So Monica was telling the truth about the dog. Perhaps Carol Ann, unable to face the fact her little companion had died, had seen the student with a dog which looked exactly like hers and convinced herself Monica had stolen him. With her history of mental illness and a sudden trigger like the death of her beloved pet, it was more than plausible that she'd fabricated the theft in her own mind and convinced herself it was true.

The obsession the dead woman had with the student had, Lilly thought, been answered, but she still had more questions. Why did Monica have a letter from Joseph to his wife? What was the motive for Carol Ann's murder? And most important of all, who had killed her?

She needed to return the pocket watch to Joseph Hotch rather than the police, she decided. Maybe she should ask him about the letter at the same time? She'd need to think about that. It would probably be better just to hand it over to the police and have done with it. She started the car and pulled out of the car park. First things first, she needed to get back to the shop.

Chapter Nine

*S*HE STOPPED BRIEFLY on the way back to town to pick up a lunch of cheese sandwiches and cartons of hot tomato and basil soup for her and Stacey. The day was warm but after her encounter with Monica she was in need of comfort food.

"Hey, you're back. And with my favourite lunch! Thank you. So, how'd it go?"

There was only one customer browsing, and she left shortly after, so they ate their lunch together at the counter and Lilly brought her up to date.

"It turns out that Carol Ann's husband is a dog breeder on the side. He gave his wife one from a litter several years ago and Monica bought hers from a more recent litter."

"So, they're not the same dog?"

"No, although they obviously look very similar. Unfortunately, Carol Ann's dog was killed by a car about a year ago. It seems the event was so traumatic she got it into her head that Monica had stolen him when she saw her with an almost identical animal."

"Man, that's really sad. Poor dog and poor Carol Ann. But at least you found the answer to the mystery."

"Yes, but it's got me nowhere. Honestly, Stacey, I don't know why I thought I could investigate this myself. I must have been out of my mind. I know my certainty that it was neither an accident nor suicide was proved right, but the post-mortem confirmed that, anyway, so what exactly have I achieved? All I've done is scare poor Monica, antagonise Joseph Hotch, and get on the wrong side of Abigail. Not to mention trespassing and petty theft. I've decided to give back the watch and photo to Carol Ann's husband and contact Bonnie about a letter I've discovered, then leave the professionals to get on with it. I am not cut out to be a detective."

"Yeah, you're probably right," Stacey said. "Don't beat yourself up about it. You did your best. Oh, head's up, we've got customers."

Lilly grabbed the empty food wrappers and made her way to the store room bin while Stacey greeted them. On her return she came face-to-face with two people she hadn't expected to see, either in her shop or together. Joseph Hotch and just behind him, Barney Darwin.

*J*OSEPH GLANCED UP and locked eyes with Lilly. "You!" he exclaimed.

Lilly gave a tentative smile. "Mr Hotch, welcome to my shop."

"Your shop?" he said, clearly surprised. "I've heard good things about the place recently. I didn't realise you owned it. I should have made the connection sooner. I was in town for lunch with a friend today, trying to take my mind off things. We decided to call in. I believe you've already met Barney Darwin?"

Oh, dear. "Yes." She nodded in the landlord's direction. He replied with a scowl.

"Can I brew you a sample of anything? I've got a green tea with Jasmine, which is a good stress reliever. Or perhaps a dandelion root. It helps to boost serotonin levels?"

He eyed her carefully. Perhaps he realised how much thought she'd put into the teas she'd just recommended? "I'll try the dandelion. Thanks."

She boiled the kettle, left it for a few minutes so it didn't scald the tea and reduce its flavour, then made a ritual of setting out the bone-china cup and saucer, brewing, timing and finally pouring the tea through a silver strainer into the cup. She slid it across the counter with a smile.

After several sips, he nodded. "I like it. I'll take some, please."

She weighed and measured two-hundred grams. Poured it into a vintage style biodegradable box filled with bleach free tissue paper and closed it with a Tea Emporium sticker. She also included one of the information leaflets.

"It's on the house, with my compliments."

"Oh, thank you. But, there's no need."

"I know, but I'd like to all the same. Mr Hotch, I owe you an apology."

"I seem to remember you already did that."

"Well, yes. But actually I have an additional confession to make."

She glanced around the shop to make sure they weren't overheard. Stacey was dealing with several customers, one of whom was piling the counter with items intended for purchase, but she glanced in Lilly's direction every so often to check on her. Others were asking questions and Barney Darwin was standing a few steps away with his back turned, studying the china cabinets.

"I really am very sorry and I hope you'll forgive me," she began in a low voice. "When you walked in on me at the flat the other day, I was holding a pocket watch I'd found. It was pure instinct when I heard your footsteps. I'm afraid I just shoved it in my pocket. I forgot all about it until I got home and I've been carrying it around ever since. I need to give it back to you. I never meant to take it in the first place."

Joseph scowled. "You know, I wasn't happy that you broke in in the first place. Now you're telling me you stole something?"

"I didn't technically break in," Lilly began.

"Yes, if I remember rightly, you said the door was unlocked. Barney, however, is convinced it wasn't. So what's the truth? Come on, Miss Tweed, considering the way you've acted recently, you owe me at least that much."

Lilly's stomach curled with anxiety. She was caught. Stacey was assisting a customer at the other side of the shop, but she was quite aware that both Joseph's tone of voice and body language had changed from politely pleasant to mildly threatening. Lilly took a deep breath. Honesty was always the best policy; she needed to own up to what she had done.

"THE TRUTH IS, after Carol Ann wrote to me, I wanted to know what happened. I thought there was more to her death, and I didn't think the police were taking things as seriously as they should. I decided to start investigating myself, which I realise now was a monumentally stupid idea. I'm not cut out to be a detective. But while I was snooping, I came across a key ring and keys. I need to return those to you as well."

"You have Carol Ann's keys?" Joseph asked sharply.

Lilly nodded. "I'm sorry. I should have returned them when I found them, but I was hoping there would be something in her flat that would point to who had killed her. I had no intention of keeping them I was simply looking for clues."

Joseph deflated. It was obvious he had no more energy left for a fight. Leaning his elbows on the counter he said, "I don't suppose I can accuse you of breaking in if you had the keys, but it was still poor behaviour. When I walked in and found a complete stranger going through my wife's things, I was livid. I shouldn't have raised my voice. I understand why you panicked. But what you did was wrong."

Lilly breathed a sigh of relief. She hadn't expected Joseph Hotch to be so tolerant. In fact, he had every right to be incredibly angry. Perhaps she hadn't given him as much credit as he deserved.

"Thank you for understanding. I know the pocket watch is worth a lot of money."

Joseph scoffed, and then whispered, "Actually it's worthless. It belonged to Carol Ann's father and his father before. She was convinced it was real and I expect at one point in time it had been. But somewhere along the line a copy was made and I expect the original was sold. I had it appraised a few years ago, and it was confirmed to be a replica. I didn't tell Carol Ann, of course, it would have broken her heart. That's if she even believed me. But it meant a lot to her, and I'd like it back."

"Of course, I'll go and get it." Lilly said, also keeping her voice low. "I must say I'm extremely relieved to know I haven't been carrying around thousands of pounds worth of watch."

She hurried into the back store room where she'd left her handbag. She felt a huge burden lift now she'd come clean. She'd been worried sick over how Joseph Hotch was going to react when she revealed she'd taken the watch, but it couldn't have gone any better.

She hurried back to a waiting Joseph and opened her bag. It was then that she remembered the letter.

Chapter Ten

*S*HE TOOK OUT the watch and put it to the side, just as the customer added several more items to her pile, practically obscuring it. She took out the letter, hesitating for a moment. "I'm really sorry to have to ask you about this," she said. "Especially when you've been so kind about everything else... but I found this letter..."

"What letter?" he asked, holding out a hand. Lilly passed it across. "I was hoping you could explain to me why you would write something like this to her?"

He took a minute to read it through, then handed it back. "I didn't write this. I don't know where you got it or who did write it, but it certainly wasn't me."

"But it's addressed to Carol Ann and signed by you?"

His face flushed an angry red. "Look, Miss Tweed, I have been very patient with you thus far, but if you are accusing me of something, then I suggest you come right out and say it."

"I'm not accusing you of anything, Mr Hotch, I'm just trying to find answers."

"Well, you're looking in the wrong place. Now, give me my wife's watch."

Lilly reached out for the watch, frantically searching in among the customer's boxes, but it was no longer there. "It's gone!" she exclaimed just as she saw Stacey hurtling through the shop.

She stared, rooted to the spot for the short time it took Stacey to launch herself at Barney, knock him into the door-jamb and throw him into an expert headlock.

"Stacey!" Lilly shrieked and bolted round the counter to the door.

"Drop it, you thief!" Stacey snapped, and Lilly spied the watch falling from Barney's meaty hand just as he had recovered his wits enough to fling Stacey to the floor.

"Barney!" Joseph shouted in shock as he rushed over.

Barney dove for the watch, but Lilly kicked it out of his reach. He responded by giving her violent shove into a stack of shelves, causing heavy tins of tea to fall and roll across the shop floor. As Barney made a second attempt to bolt for the door, Stacey grabbed an errant tin and flung it at his head. It made impact causing him to stagger into another shelf upsetting a display of teapots. One fell and shattered with a sound like gunfire. This was the final straw for poor Earl who bolted from the window, hackles raised, hissing and snarling in fear.

"You stupid..." but before Barney could finish, Joseph grabbed the watch and savagely kicked Barney in the knee, sending him down. Earl leapt towards Barney's face, claws out, leaving a long scratch down his cheek as he used his head as a jumping off point, before fleeing to the back store room in terror.

"Stupid Cat!" Barney shrieked, reaching for the laceration, his hand coming away covered in blood.

Joseph threw his friend to the floor, putting a knee on his back, and glowered at Lilly.

"Call the police," he demanded.

*   *   *

LILLY TELEPHONED THE police and then went to check on Earl. He had calmed down and was curled up in the bed Stacey had made for him.

"When done, Earl," Lilly said, stroking his head. "Salmon for tea, I think. You deserve it."

Back in the shop, the customers who had witnessed the entire thing were being taken care of by Stacey. She'd brewed them all a calming tea and had rung up and packaged their purchases, ready for when they would be allowed to leave. All of them were more than happy to wait and give witness statements.

Lilly wandered over to where Joseph was still guarding Barney and Stacey joined them a moment later.

"I saw him take the watch right off the counter and try to walk out with it," she said.

"Are you all right?" Lilly asked, concerned. "You took a nasty fall."

"So did you. But, yeah, I'm fine."

"Well, please don't make a habit of tackling shoplifters, my heart nearly stopped."

Stacey laughed. "Sorry. I didn't really think about it, just acted. I hate thieves."

The police car arrived a moment later and Bonnie got out, walking over to the shop with a stern look on her face.

"Oh, Bonnie, I'm so glad it's you."

"What happened? Is everyone all right?"

"Yes, we're all fine. This man tried to steal a watch and Stacey tackled him. It got a bit fraught. He knocked both Stacey and me down and frightened Earl, who scratched his face." Lilly succinctly explained.

"Well, I'll need to take statements from everyone. So I suggest you put the closed sign up and lock the door." She turned to her colleague and spoke in hushed tones. He nodded, handcuffed Barney and put in him in the back of the police car before taking a seat behind the wheel to wait for Bonnie.

"Right. I take it these people are your customers who happened to be here at the time, is that correct?" Bonnie said, gesturing to the end of the counter.

"Yes. They were happy to wait to give you their statements."

"I'll start with them so they can be on their way, then come back and speak to you three."

Lilly, Stacey, and Joseph sipped newly brewed drinks at the other end of the counter while Bonnie went about her job.

"I'm sorry about your friend," Lilly said to Joseph.

"I don't understand it. He obviously knew about the watch, but why attempt to steal it?"

"He must have overheard me telling you that I had it. But he missed the bit when you told me it was a fake."

"Is that what this has all been about? A damned pocked watch?"

Lilly had no time to answer as Bonnie chose that moment to join them.

"You can let your customers out now, Lilly. I've got what I need for the moment. We'll take full statements at their homes. I've made them promise not to talk to anyone about what happened for the time being."

Lilly looked out of the window and saw there was quite a crowd gathered outside. Word had obviously spread quickly. She sighed, it wouldn't be long before a reporter was on the scene.

"Stacey, could you let everyone out then lock the door?"

"Sure."

"I think I know why he stole the watch," Joseph said to Bonnie. "Miss Tweed, was about to return it to me and he overheard part of our conversation."

"And you are?"

"Oh, sorry. Joseph Hotch."

Bonnie was brought up short. "Carol Ann's husband?" she asked, giving Lilly a brief sideways glance.

"That's right. Barney was my wife's landlord. We were separated. Barney was supposed to be keeping an eye on her for me."

"You think your wife told her landlord about the watch?"

"She must have done, officer. He wouldn't have known about it otherwise. I certainly didn't tell him."

"I'm afraid this changes everything. It's possibly connected in some way to the death of your wife, Mr Hotch, and as such will need to be passed on to the lead detective. It's not my case. I will take Miss Pepper's statement now, but then I'm afraid the two of you will have to come to the station to be interviewed. Would you like me to send a car?" Bonnie directed this last question to Lilly, who shook her head.

"No, I can drive us both. The last thing we need is to be seen driving off in the back of a police car. Is that all right with you, Mr Hotch?"

"Yes. I don't have transport with me; we came in Barney's car."

"Stacey, can you hold the fort here until I return? There's no need to open if you don't feel up to it. I expect the place will end up full of people who are just being nosy and wanting to know what's happened rather than serious shoppers."

Stacey grinned. "And that's a perfect time to sell them something," she said. "Don't worry, I'll be fine."

Fifteen minutes later, with a certain amount of trepidation, Lilly and Joseph were on their way to the police station.

❦

AT THE POLICE station they gave their names to the desk sergeant and were shown to a small waiting area. Windowless and devoid of personality, Lilly found it gloomy and depressing. The chairs were grey plastic and very uncomfortable and there was nothing in the way of reading material, unless you counted the dramatic crime posters on a nearby notice board. Joseph sat morose and silent, nursing a vending machine coffee that looked like sludge. Eventually he leaned forward and deposited the untouched paper cup on the scarred table in front of him.

He reached into his pocket and brought out the watch, turning it over in his hands as though seeing it for the first time. "Of all the stupid things... is this really the reason my wife was killed?" Lilly knew better than to interrupt. He was speaking more to himself than to her. "She reported Barney to the police before. I didn't believe her."

Lilly's mind went back to the day she had hit Abigail's car. After Bonnie had sent her on her way, they'd both talked about Carol Ann. She recalled Bonnie mentioning that she'd reported Barney to the police for breaking into her flat. Barney had naturally denied it, and as there was no proof it had been put down to Carol Ann's mental illness and increased paranoia.

"You knew she'd called the police about Barney?"

"Yes. First time it happened they brought him here, and he called me." Joseph said. "I came down here straight away and talked to the police, explained the situation about how my wife was ill, delusional. At the time, I thought I was just cleaning up another one of her messes. I didn't think for one minute that Barney had actually broken into her flat. This whole time I thought he was looking out for her."

Lilly tried to reassure him. "At the risk of repeating myself, you can't blame yourself. Given her history, it makes sense that you'd believe Barney, especially as there was no proof and that Carol Ann may not have been taking her pills."

Joseph slipped the watch back into his pocket. "All over a stupid watch, which isn't even the real thing, just a clever copy."

"Yes, but Barney didn't know that, did he? He thought it was worth a lot of money. How did you and Barney meet?"

"I used to breed small dogs and his niece wanted one. He came to me. It was years ago, but we kind of became loose friends after that. Occasional drinks at the local pub, a couple of football games, that sort of thing. We weren't best friends, but we were close enough that he called me when Carol Ann showed up wanting to rent one of his flats. She didn't know Barney, you see, and wasn't aware we knew each other. I thought it was the perfect way to... well... give myself a bit of a break while simultaneously giving her some independence, and with someone to watch out for her in case she needed help. Someone who could also keep me informed about how she was doing. And to think he was taking advantage all this time! It sickens me to my stomach, it really does."

"I really am sorry about what's happened," Lilly said. "Especially my part in it all. I got rather sucked into it after Carol Ann wrote to me. I should have just left well alone and let the police do their job."

"Well, if it wasn't for you we wouldn't have caught Barney," Joseph replied.

"Does this mean you forgive me for taking the watch?"

He shrugged. "I suppose it must."

From the corner of her eye, Lilly spotted movement. She glanced over and saw Bonnie enter the hall from a door at the back marked private. She made her way towards them, a stern look on her face.

*B*OTH LILLY AND Joseph stood up instinctively, leaning forward in anticipation of what news Bonnie had to tell them.

"What did he say?" asked Lilly.

"Has he confessed?" said Joseph at the same time.

Bonnie held up both hands to halt the onslaught of questions before they came. She took a seat opposite and turned a page in her notebook. Lilly and Joseph sat back down and waited for her to speak.

"No, he hasn't confessed as such. He's adamant he had nothing to do with the death of your wife, Mr Hotch, although at this stage I wouldn't expect him to admit to any involvement. He's keeping tight lipped in that regard but has given us an alibi for the time, which we are in the process of checking now. However, he has made an interesting admission about the watch."

"Oh?" Joseph said.

"He says he bought the watch from Carol Ann, but after he'd paid, she refused to give it to him."

"Then he's lying. Carol Ann would *never* have sold that watch, it meant too much to her."

"Did he break into her flat looking for it, then?" asked Lilly. "Is that what Carol Ann meant? Her letter to me said she was sure someone else had been in her home while she'd been out."

Bonnie nodded. "Yes, he's admitted to entering her flat while she was out. On a couple of occasions in the early hours she was actually there and caught him. Several times he entered, apparently, looking for the watch he's adamant he bought from her. He couldn't find it, though."

"That despicable... is there any proof he paid for the watch?" Joseph asked. "Did you find a receipt or a note or anything? We have a joint bank account so I can check the statements if that's any help?"

"He said he paid cash."

Joseph threw up his hands in despair. "Well, of course he did! It's just a web of lies to try to get himself off the hook."

"How much did he say he'd paid for it?" Lilly asked.

"Five-hundred pounds."

Lilly glanced at Joseph, wondering if he realised the implication. He was frowning, but she wasn't sure if he'd put two and two together as yet. His mind was probably clouded with anger at the thoughts of Barney Darwin entering his wife's home while she slept.

"He's even more of a louse than I thought he was then." She said, eventually. "Carol Ann thought the pocket watch was the genuine article and would have told Barney so. He therefore thought it was worth thousands, yet only offered a meager five-hundred for it. He was taking advantage of and hoping to profit from a very ill woman."

"That utter..." Joseph swore loudly, then jumped up and began to pace from one side of the small area to the other. "That's his motive, isn't it? He killed my wife because she wouldn't give him the blasted watch. He had plenty of opportunity to work it all out because they lived in the same building. A building he owned and had all the spare keys for. Gain her trust and slowly make her think she was going mad, then make himself the one who she'd turn to. Dear god, I should have believed her." He returned to his seat, dashing away tears before they could fall.

"What about his alibi, Bonnie?"

"Lilly, I can't really discuss that with you. Suffice to say we're following it up, but it's a bit shaky."

"Okay. But off the record, do you think Barney killed Carol Ann?"

Bonnie stood up and Lilly did the same. Joseph remained sitting, emotionally exhausted, but likewise interested in what Bonnie's answer would be.

"It's not my call, Lilly, you know that. This isn't my case. But, off the record, I think we've probably got our man. He clearly had a motive and as her landlord would have known her routine. As you said, Mr Hotch, he would have been able to spend the time gaining her trust and alienating her from her friends and family. But, you both know as well as I do that none of this means anything unless we can prove it."

Lilly nodded. "Yes, of course."

"All right. I need to go back in now. I only came to double check whether Carol Ann would have willingly sold the watch. Someone will be with you in the next fifteen minutes or so to take a formal statement."

After Bonnie had gone, Lilly sat back down and turned to Joseph. "Are you all right?"

He shook his head. "I don't know. I trusted someone who I thought was a friend to look out for my wife. Now it looks as though he not only took advantage of her, but probably killed her. I've got so many different emotions warring with each other that all I can feel is a numb shock."

"Can I get you anything from the machine? Tea or coffee or something to eat?"

"No, I couldn't stomach a thing, thanks."

"Look, Joseph, I know this is a bad time, but I need to ask you about the letter?"

"Letter? What letter?"

Lilly rooted around in her bag and brought out the letter she'd found when she'd spoken to Monica.

"I'd forgotten all about that," he said wearily. "But, I told you I didn't write it. It's not my writing, look." He brought out his wallet and showed Lilly several examples of his writing. On a cheque, a shopping list and his signature on the back of his credit card. It didn't match the letter.

"Well, someone did, and we need to find out who. Because it makes you look culpable."

"*D*O YOU THINK Barney could have written it?" Joseph said.

"Barney?"

"Yes, to implicate me?"

"No, I don't think so. I found it at St John's. One of the students there had it, a girl called Monica Morris. You know her, I think?"

"No, I don't... oh, wait, yes, she had one of my puppies. I used to breed Pomeranians, and she took one from me, Pipsqueak. It was a while ago now, though."

"This one?" Lilly asked, pulling out the photograph of Monica with her dog.

Joseph stared at it for a moment before letting out an uncomfortable sigh. "Where did you get this?"

"Your wife's flat," she replied, handing it to him. "It belongs to you now. I had heard Carol Ann was upset when she saw Monica with her dog?"

"I don't know anything about that. She was grief stricken because her own dog had been killed by a car. Maybe she thought this dog was hers. What was she doing with this photo?"

"How did you and Monica meet?"

"At a reunion at St John's. The three of us, that's Carol Ann, Monica and myself, got talking and the conversation turned to dogs. I said I bred them and she wanted one. That's it really."

"You didn't meet up at all, other than when she collected her dog? Socialise maybe?"

"No, we did not. I had no contact with her after she took the dog and I don't think I like what you're implying, Miss Tweed. They've caught the man who murdered my wife, and I really think you should stop with the amateur sleuthing. Just leave it to the professionals before you make things worse."

Lilly didn't have a response to that. He was right, she needed to let this whole investigation go and get on with her own life. Joseph Hotch was under enough strain already without her making it worse. With perfect timing, a police constable came through to escort them to separate interview rooms and they said their goodbye's.

Almost an hour later Lilly had completed her statement and made her way back to the reception area. There was no sign of Joseph Hotch. He had either left before she had or was still being interviewed. It was probably for the best, Lilly thought.

She glanced at her phone and saw a text from Stacey confirming they'd had a great number of people in the shop after she'd left. A record day for sales, but she'd not breathed a word about what had happened. She'd apparently locked up and left Earl asleep in the window. After a short time in the back room, he'd decided it was safe to venture back out to his favourite spot.

In the car on the return journey, Lilly's mind wouldn't rest. There was something Joseph Hotch had said that was important. Something that didn't seem quite right, but try as she might, she couldn't remember what it was. She decided to do something totally unrelated to the case. Forget all about it in fact and hope her subconscious would do the work. It would come to her, eventually. And she had the perfect project to keep her mind busy.

Chapter Eleven

SHE MADE A quick detour on her way back to the shop to visit fellow trader Jim Carmichael. He owned the DIY and hardware shop on the outskirts of the market square. The shop sign was turned to closed, but peering through the glass-fronted door she could see him still at the counter. She knocked and waved as he looked up.

"Lilly, what a nice surprise. Come on in."

"Hi, Jim, sorry to turn up so late, it's been a bit of a rush today."

"No problem. I'm in the middle of a stock take so will be here for a while yet." He locked the door behind her and they made their way to the small kitchenette at the back. "I was just making a cup of tea. Do you want one?"

"No, I'm fine thanks, Jim. I've come for some paint, actually."

"Then you're in the right place, but don't tell me you're doing up the shop again?"

"No, that's perfect as it is. It's for the flat above. I'm renting it out to Stacey, the girl who works for me, but it could do with a bit of an upgrade."

"Any ideas about colours? I've got a good range, but if you want something in particular, I can mix it for you. Shouldn't take long."

Lilly gave him the colours she was thinking of and between them they looked at what was available on the shelves. None were quite what Lilly had in mind, though.

"You know, for the age of the building I think you wouldn't go far wrong with the heritage range." Jim said, handing her a colour chart.

"Oh, these are perfect." She said, indicating the two colours she had been thinking of.

They spent the next ten minutes choosing everything else Lilly would need, including rollers, paint trays, brushes and paint for the ceiling and woodwork.

"Okay, I'll get this lot sorted out for you and deliver it to the back door in about an hour with the invoice. How's that sound?"

"Perfect. Thanks, Jim, I appreciate it."

On the way out, he asked her about the trouble at the shop earlier in the day.

"You heard about that did you?"

"It was the talk of the town all afternoon. You're all right though, are you?"

"I'm fine. It was a case of opportunistic theft, that's all. It just got a little heated, but Bonnie came and sorted it out.

I don't think he'll bother us again." Lilly said, not wanting, nor in fact able, as per the police order, to give too much detail. No doubt the full story would come to light in the coming days.

"That's a relief to know. Right, I better get on with your order. See you shortly."

Back at the shop, Earl raised his head as soon as he heard the key in the door and came to weave himself round Lilly's legs when she entered. She scooped him up and gave him a cuddle.

"Well, Earl, what an exciting day you had," she said to the purring cat. "Glad to see you're back to your usual self."

She popped him on the counter while she read the brief note Stacey had left. She'd cleaned up the breakages, re-stocked those items she'd sold and balanced the till, putting the days takings in the safe. Lilly checked the total on the till receipt and was amazed. It had been the best day she'd had since she'd opened, and that included the launch day. It was amazing what a bit of drama could do. It looked as though everyone who set foot through the door to gossip had been sold something by Stacey. The girl really was an excellent salesperson.

"Come on Earl, let's go and see about getting the flat sorted out. But first a treat for you."

She always kept a few tins of tuna or salmon in the staff kitchen for Earl, just in case. Having filled up his bowls, she left him to it and exited the back door in time to see Jim drive up with a car full of decorating supplies. Unlocking the door, he helped her carry everything upstairs to the flat.

Jim looked around, and then nodded. "The paint is a very good choice for this place. It will be beautiful when it's finished. It's good to see all the original features are still here, too," he said, indicating the ornate coving, ceiling rose and picture rail. "So many of these old places have been stripped of their history. Right, I'll leave you to it, Lilly. Give me a call if you need anything else."

"I will. Thanks, Jim."

Alone, Lilly sent a quick text to Stacey thanking her for her hard work, then rolled up her sleeves, snapped on rubber gloves and set to scrubbing the place from top to bottom. Time to make the place sparkle.

W HEN SHE'D BOUGHT the building, the upstairs flat had been in reasonably good condition, just neglected. It was clean, though dusty, but there was no water damage as the roof had been repaired by the previous owner and the old sash windows were in excellent condition. There was also some furniture; a double bed base, wardrobe and chest of drawers in the bedroom. A small dining table and two chairs in the kitchen and two wing back armchairs in the lounge. It was certainly enough for Stacey who had no furniture of her own. Lilly would purchase a mattress for the bed and she had a few pairs of spare curtains at the cottage she could use.

She was up the ladder cleaning the glass shade in the bathroom when her phone rang. It was Stacey.

"Hey, Lilly, just got your message. It was a great day after you left, so many people came in to find out what was going on."

"It looks like they all went away with something too."

"Yeah. Although it wasn't difficult to sell anything, they loved everything you have. I definitely think we got quite a few new regular customers out of it. So how'd you get on with the police?"

"Not much to tell, really. We gave our statements, and that was it. We didn't see Barney at all. Are you okay after your fall?"

"I'm fine. It looked worse than it was. Where are you, it sounds really echoey?"

"I'm up a ladder in the flat bathroom. Hang on, I'll move to the lounge."

"Wait, are you cleaning up there? I'll come and help if you want?"

"Okay, if you're sure? That would be a great help. Do you need a lift?"

"No, I've just got my car back. It was the fan belt, so all fixed now. I'll see you soon."

Lilly had finished in the bathroom and was already half-way through scrubbing the kitchen when Stacey turned up. She didn't see her but heard a squeal and a moment later she came rushing in. "You bought paint! And my favourite colours. Thank you so much, Lilly."

"It needed painting anyway, so I may as well use the colours you like as you're the one moving in. It's going to look great when it's finished."

"I can't wait. Right, let me get to work in the living room."

An industrious two hours later and the whole place was clean and ready for the new paint. It was too late, and they were too tired to begin decorating, so Lilly suggested a cup of tea in the shop to wind down before going home. "I need to get Earl, anyway."

Over a hot cup of Chamomile infused with lemon balm, the discussion inevitably turned to Carol Ann Hotch and Barney Darwin's part in her death.

"So, he murdered her just so he could have her watch?" Stacey said incredulously.

"He said he bought the watch from her and she wouldn't give it to him even though she'd taken his money. But I suppose it amounts to the same thing."

"You don't believe he bought it?"

"No, I don't. There's no proof he gave her any money, and he's admitted sneaking into her flat to try to take it. From what I can understand, he entered when she was asleep and woke her up a couple of times. Poor woman must have been scared out of her wits when she saw him."

"Man, that is all kinds of messed up. What a worm."

"I think he was intent on stealing the watch, but whether he killed her for it, I can't say. There's no proof of that either at the moment. Then there's this letter I found, which doesn't fit in with anything so far."

"What letter?"

"I found it at St John's when I was speaking with Monica. Written to Carol Ann by Joseph, but he denied writing it, and when we checked his handwriting, it wasn't a match. But who did write it, and why did Monica have it?"

"Yeah, that seems strange. What did Monica say?"

"I haven't spoken to her about it yet. I slipped it out of her bag when she left."

Stacey smirked. "Cat burglar Tweed strikes again."

"Embarrassingly, yes." Lilly admitted with a wry smile. "But I won't be doing it again."

"Well, the only one who can answer your questions is Monica."

Lilly nodded in agreement. "I'm not looking forward to it considering how we left things, but I'll need to visit her one last time if I want answers."

"I thought you were going to let the police deal with it from now on?"

"So did I, Stacey. In fact, Bonnie told me to do just that. But I need to find answers to my questions, otherwise I just won't be able to sleep. I'm honestly not sure if they've got the right man. And if they haven't, then we need to find the right one."

Chapter Twelve

THE FOLLOWING MORNING, after helping Stacey get the shop up and running, Lilly headed back to the university with the intention of having another conversation with Monica about the letter. She didn't suspect Monica of having anything to do with Carol Ann's death, but it was very odd that she had a forged letter from the deceased's husband in her bag.

Perhaps someone had slipped it in there without her knowing to make her look culpable? It was practically common knowledge that Carol Ann was fixated on Monica, so it wouldn't take much of a stretch of imagination to point a guilty finger at her and make people believe it. But who would be in a position to do such a thing?

She drove on, lost in thought. It was a beautiful day with real warmth in the spring sunshine and the bright yellow heads of newly opened daffodils swaying in the gentle breeze. But Lilly hardly noticed. She had so many other things on her mind. The police may be confident they had their suspect in custody and part of her knew she should just let it go, but her stubborn side insisted there was more to find and Barney's motive seemed absurd to her.

Whoever had killed Carol Ann had done their research, they knew about her medications, her mental illness. Which, admittedly, Barney also did, but they had been smart enough to make it look like an accident or suicide. There had been some clever thought behind it and Barney, to her mind at least, didn't seem clever enough to have committed the crime. He'd tried to steal the watch in broad daylight in front of several people, for heaven's sake.

Plus, if he knew she was already dead, then he'd had plenty of time to enter the flat and find the watch before the police turned up. He could even have taken the safe out of the wardrobe. It was quite heavy, admittedly, but it wasn't large and not bolted in place. He could have taken it away on a dolly trolley to work on at his leisure. Carol Ann resided on the ground floor so it would have been easy enough, then he could have spent some time trying to get inside before returning it.

Let's face it, Barney not only owned the building but he lived in it. As landlord he legitimately could enter the other resident's homes without raising suspicion. If he had covered up the safe and wheeled it around the building to his own ground floor flat would anyone have raised an eyebrow? Lilly thought not. She shook her head. The more she thought about it, the less sense it made.

She parked and was halfway to the accommodation block when she realised Monica would most likely be in class. She changed direction and took a seat at a bench under the shade of an oak tree, halfway between the classrooms and G block. Hopefully Monica would pass this way and she would be able to intercept her.

Quarter of an hour later she was just about to give up when a flood of students poured out of the main building. Lilly scanned the crowd and almost at the end of the sea of people spotted Monica leaving the chemistry lab and walking towards her, head down, looking at her phone. She had a backpack across one shoulder and in her free hand carried her hockey stick.

Lilly stood just as she reached her. "Monica."

The girl glanced up, her mild expression changing to one of disgust as she realised who it was. "Oh no, not you again. What do you want now? Why can't you just leave me alone?" She shoved her phone in her pocket and strode away down the path. Lilly hurried along beside her.

"Actually, I've come with some news. I thought you'd be interested to know that the police have someone in custody for Carol Ann's murder."

"What?" she said, coming to a sudden halt. "That was quick. Who was it? Do you know?"

"It's not important because I think they have the wrong person and they're going to realise it soon."

"So, you still think you're better than police? Can't you see how arrogant you sound?"

Lilly ignored the jibe and continued. "There are some things which don't add up, and I think you can help me fill in the gaps. I know Carol Ann discussed you regularly with her therapist and the general opinion was that she was obsessed with you for no reason. You thought that too."

"I still think that."

"When I first talked to you, you acted like you hardly knew Carol Ann or her husband, yet you had one of his puppies and were able to personally message him when his wife broke into G block."

"So?"

Lilly's stomach suddenly flipped over as she remembered that elusive comment of Joseph's which she'd failed to grasp the importance of at the time.

"You said it took a while to name Pipsqueak. You didn't name her straight away. Joseph Hotch told me once you'd taken her home you and he never saw each other again."

"We didn't. What is this all about?"

"When I showed him the photograph of you and your dog I got from Carol Ann's flat, he knew your dog's name immediately. How would he know that unless you'd been in touch?"

"I don't know, maybe he saw me around here with her. It's not a secret what I called her."

"Perhaps, but I don't think so, Monica. Then there's this letter." Lilly pulled the letter out of her pocket. "This letter, supposedly from Joseph to his wife, was in your bag. But the thing is I compared it to Joseph's handwriting. It's not his."

Monica snatched the letter from Lilly's hand and looked at it. "You stole this from my bag! I ought to call the police right now."

"I agree. Go ahead," Lilly said. "Because I know you're the one who wrote the letter, Monica. I feel stupid for not noticing it before, but that's your handwriting. I saw it on the clipboard the day we met and it matches perfectly. The question is why did you forge this letter to Carol Ann?"

"You're as crazy as she was. I didn't write this!" Monica shouted. "And I'm calling security right now."

Lilly took a step back as Monica raised her hockey stick. If she didn't try to calm her down, things could get very nasty. Then she saw a familiar face coming to her rescue for a second time. Frederick Warren reached out and gently pushed Monica's arm down, lowering the stick. "Monica, what's going on? What are you shouting about?"

Monica prodded a finger at Lilly. "This crazy woman stole something from my bag and is now accusing me of stuff I didn't do."

"Are you sure, Monica, it seems a bit unlikely?"

"What? You're accusing me of lying?" she hissed at him, eyes flashing dangerously.

"No, of course I'm not, but you can't just go around accusing people of stealing, Monica. Maybe you should go back to halls and calm down, all right?"

"I wasn't the one bothering her!" Monica spat, but Frederick stood his ground. "Fine! Take her side." Monica yelled at him then stormed away.

Fred stood for a moment staring after Monica, a look of concern on his face. Then he turned back to Lilly. "What was that about, Miss Tweed? You seem to get into trouble a lot around here."

"Thank you, Fred," Lilly said. "That's the second time you've rescued me from a heated discussion. Hard as it probably is to believe, I'm not the type who goes looking for trouble."

Fred gave a grim smile in response, then looked down and kicked an errant stone across the path into the grass. "Look, Miss Tweed," he said, a slightly irritated note in his voice. "I appreciate the advice you gave me, and I don't want to sound rude, but you needn't be concerned about my private life. It's all sorted out now."

"Fred, I'm sorry, but I have no idea what you're talking about."

Fred blinked in confusion. "Monica," he said. "She's my ex-girlfriend."

LILLY SPENT A few minutes reassuring Fred that her reason for speaking with Monica was totally unrelated to her being his ex, then phone in hand and heart pounding as she realised how things were fitting together she raced back to her car, dialling Archie's number as she went. She'd had all the clues and couldn't believe it had taken her so long to work it out.

She briefly wondered if phoning Bonnie rather than Archie would be better, but then dismissed the idea. Bonnie had told her that she should leave the investigation to the police and not get involved. If she went to her now, she'd be admitting she hadn't taken any notice. There was also the matter that if she were proved wrong, and realistically that could very well be the case, then she'd be wasting Bonnie's time. Archie was well placed to do some semi-official investigation work and could then pass his findings onto Bonnie himself. This seemed to Lilly to be the best plan all round. Unfortunately, Archie wasn't answering his phone. She left a brief message.

"Archie, it's Lilly. I need you to call me back as soon as you get this. I've just discovered something important regarding Carol Ann Hotch's murder. I'm almost sure they've got the wrong person. I'd like your input on what I've found out. Please, call me as soon as you can."

She hung up, turned round and came face to face with Abigail Douglas.

"Abigail."

"Lillian. So, you've got a lead in the murder case, have you?" she asked, nostrils flaring. "What are you doing still investigating? You don't work for the newspaper anymore, nor are you a private detective. None of this is any of your business, yet you still insist on poking your nose where it doesn't belong."

"And you know what, Abigail? I could say the same about you. You're supposed to be the paper's agony aunt, so what are you doing following this story?"

"Trying to keep a roof over my head! It's all right for you, you've got a successful business, but what about me? Thanks to you no one is writing in to the paper anymore and..." she stopped suddenly, choking on her words as tears pooled. She grabbed a hankie from her pocket, dabbed her eyes and blew her nose.

Lilly was shocked at Abigail's sudden vulnerability. She was such a stony and inflexible woman normally. Pecksniffian her mother would have called her. But on closer inspection she realised there were telltale signs that things were obviously very wrong. The smear of mascara on her cheek, the silver roots showing in her normally perfect coiffure, and the red lipstick on her front tooth.

"Abigail, are you all right?"

She shook her head and sniffed. "No, not really. They're talking about getting rid of my agony aunt column. If I can't transition to something else, it will be too late. I'll be out of a job."

"I'm sorry to hear that," Lilly said.

"I uprooted myself for this job, you know? Gave up everything and now, just a few months later, it looks like it's all been for nothing. And worse, I've nowhere else to go. I've been following the Carol Ann Hotch case closely. Doing my due diligence, following up sources in the hope that if I write a good story, I'll be able to prove to the editors that I know what I'm doing. But no matter what I do you get there first. Please, Lilly, it's not your job, but it's everything to me. My last chance. Would you please share what you know with me?"

Lilly stared dumbstruck for a moment. She didn't recognise this contrite, apologetic and polite Abigail. Things must be really bad at the paper. However, she felt she should really be providing this information to Archie, not only because he was her friend but because he was the newspaper's official crime reporter. She didn't owe this woman anything. Still, a part of her felt somewhat responsible for the shaky predicament Abigail now found herself in.

"Okay," Lilly said at last. "I'll help you, but you must promise me something first."

"What?"

"Before you write one word, you must share what I'm about to tell you with Archie. In fact, you could partner on the article as Archie has also been working on it. Longer than you or me actually, so he deserves this break as much, if not more than anyone. Do you promise to tell him everything?"

"Yes, all right," Abigail said, albeit a little reluctantly. "I suppose it's the right thing to do."

"Okay. Well, I'd rather not discuss this in the university car park, there's a cafe not far from here where we can talk."

"Good idea. I could do with a strong cup of coffee. You can drive and then drop me back off here to collect my car. Seems silly to take two, don't you think, what with the price of petrol nowadays."

Lilly rolled her eyes at Abigail's audacity. Then again, having seen already how carelessly she drove, did she really want to be a passenger with her behind the wheel? The answer was a resounding no. She unlocked the mini and invited Abigail into the passenger seat. Hoping the conversation wouldn't be reduced to a slanging match. You could never tell how things would pan out with Abigail Douglas.

HOLLINGBECK FARM WAS about a mile outside St John's university on the top moorland road with views of Plumpton Mallet nestled in the valley below. A working dairy farm, the owners, Judith and Richard Fosdyke, had diversified when the price of milk had fallen below sustainable levels.

The conversion of a long, low stone barn to a cafe and restaurant had taken nearly a year once planning had been approved and had become an almost instant success. Popular with walkers, hikers and cyclists in particular, it catered for special events such as birthdays and weddings as well. It was also one of the local outlets that sold Lilly's tea in their cafe.

"I didn't know this was here," Abigail said to Lilly as they exited their vehicles. "It's got awards too. Look at those plaques on the wall."

"Yes, it's very popular. There's a lovely garden at the back which will give us some privacy."

The entrance to the rear garden was through the main cafe and as they made their way past tables, the majority of which were full, a jolly looking woman in a floral apron waved at Lilly from behind the counter. "Lilly, I didn't know you were coming today. How are you?"

"I'm well thank you, Judy." She introduced Abigail and explained they were looking for a quiet place in the garden.

"Of course, you go right ahead. I'll send Bethany out with a menu shortly."

Out of earshot Abigail hissed, "Do you know every-one, Lillian?"

"Not quite. See that man over there in the corner?"

Abigail peered in the direction Lilly indicated. "Yes?"

"Well, I don't know him."

"Oh, very droll."

Over tea and toasted crumpets underneath an arbour which provided both shelter and privacy, Lilly laid some ground rules.

"Firstly, what I'm about to tell you is only what I have discovered and put together myself. There's no evidence as such. You won't be able to use a lot of it before it's proved otherwise you could find yourself in court. Again."

Abigail ignored the thinly veiled reference to her previously close call with the local courts, but her face flushed angrily.

"I'm familiar with both the libel and slander laws, Lillian. I wouldn't dream of writing anything which could get either myself or the paper in trouble. Now, tell me what you know."

Lilly replenished their tea, then began with how Frederick Warren had turned up at the shop one day worried about his pregnant girlfriend.

"The young man who was so rude to me?"

"He wasn't rude to you, Abigail, but yes, that's him."

"So, he got his girlfriend pregnant."

"No, someone else did. She was having an affair with a married man. I didn't realise who Fred's girlfriend was until just now at the university, although I should have done. The clues were there. She offered me a ginger sweet when I first met her, which helps with morning sickness. And there were vitamins in her bag."

"So, who was the married man?"

"I think it was Joseph Hotch."

"Carol Ann's husband!" Abigail squeaked. "Oh my word, this changes things. How do you know? And who is the girl?"

"It's Monica Morris."

"The one Carol Ann was obsessed with? Of course! I spoke to her before. Although thanks to you getting in there first, it took all my powers of persuasion to get the most meagre details from her."

Lilly bit her tongue, ignoring the jibe. She was determined not to rise to the woman's barbs. Abigail continued, scanning her notebook.

"I managed to confirm she adopted a puppy from Joseph Hotch a while ago. Told me she met him at one of the reunions."

"That's right. No one knows she's pregnant, so tread very lightly with that information."

"So, what exactly is your theory, Lilly?"

"Joseph has an affair with Monica. I don't know when it started, not long after they met and she got her puppy, I would think. Carol Ann in her letter to me said she thought he was having an affair. She left him and moved out to a flat of her own. On account of the affair, or for some other reason, I don't know. Regardless, the affair carries on and Monica ends up pregnant. Joseph doesn't know she is by the way, but Fred found out and after a heart-to-heart chat they decide to break up. Monica then realises she's going to be on her own when the baby comes and it's a frightening thought. She's young and scared, understandably, but Joseph has already ended the affair as he wants to reconcile with his wife. Carol Ann is the one thing standing in the way of a proper relationship with Joseph and a future for her and the baby."

"Oh, gosh, Lilly. You think Monica killed Carol Ann?"

Lilly nodded. "I find it very difficult to believe, but it's beginning to look that way, isn't it?"

"But how? The autopsy report said she was drugged, causing a fatal overdose."

"Do you remember the story you wrote about the break-in and theft at the laboratory at St John's?"

"Of course."

"Can you remember what was stolen?"

"A number of high value apparatus which I can't remember the names of, those small enough to carry away at least. The place was completely ransacked, so it was difficult to piece together exactly what was missing for ages. But there was a lot of pharmaceuticals taken... Oh dear, yes, now I see where you're heading. You really think Monica was smart enough to do this?"

"Her major is pharmaceuticals, Abigail, she spends a lot of time in the labs studying. She knows them like the back of her hand. She'd know when they would be empty, the codes for the doors and the locks on the cupboards. I also think she'd be clever enough to take a multitude of items and an array of different drugs in order to camouflage what she really intended to steal. It would be difficult to connect the murder with the theft at the lab then. The only point I'm not sure of is the fact that Fred broke up with her *after* the robbery, so that would mean she was planning the murder for quite a while before she suddenly found herself single."

"Maybe..." Abigail began, tapping her pen against her teeth while she thought. "She was sure her boyfriend would dump her when he found out she was pregnant?"

"Yes, that's a distinct possibility. Fred, told me they'd never slept together, Monica wanted to wait apparently, so there's no way the baby could have been his."

"Mmm. But do you really think she was deciding to kill Carol Ann so far in advance?"

"Honestly? I don't know. But why else would she steal the drugs?"

Abigail snapped her fingers and immediately went into reporter mode. Speaking in headlines. "Desperate times call for desperate measures. A young, single student with bright prospects finds herself pregnant by a married man, who has already hinted his intention of returning to his wife, and suddenly her future is in ruins. Penniless, shunned by her parents and unable to find a job. What would you do for money?"

"You think she was planning on selling the stolen drugs?"

"I do. It's what I originally wrote in my article, if you remember."

This thought had not occurred to Lilly, but she could see it held some not insignificant merit. "You know, I think you might be right, Abigail. Monica knew she would be needing money, so stole drugs with a high street value that could be easily sold on. But when Fred broke it off with her and Joseph decided to try again with his wife, she was suddenly alone. She decided to use the resources she already had at her disposal to get rid of Carol Ann, leaving the way clear for her and Joseph to have a future, especially when she told him about the baby."

Abigail grinned and snapped her notebook shut. "Excellent work if I say so myself. Now I've just got write it."

"You'll need more than just speculation before you put anything in print, Abigail. All we've managed to do is talk through our ideas, putting them together with what we already know and making them fit the crime. It's not enough. There needs to be definitive proof. And don't forget to let Archie know what we've discussed. That was the deal, remember?"

"Of course, dear. Now, I'll just go and pay a visit to the powder room. I'll meet you back at the car."

Typical, Lilly thought as she watched Abigail sashay her way back inside. *Leave me with the bill.* But she couldn't be bothered to argue.

⚬⚬⚬

THE RETURN JOURNEY saw Abigail back to her usual tactless and slightly acerbic self, and Lilly switched off. By the time she pulled into the university car park, she'd just about had enough. Then they saw Abigail's car.

"My car!" she screamed. "Look at my car. It's only just been fixed!"

The windscreen had been smashed along with both wing mirrors and there was a huge dent in the bonnet. Lilly and Abigail jumped out of the mini and rushed over.

"Who would do such a wicked thing!"

The answer came almost instantly and Lilly just had time to yell, "Look out!" and grab Abigail's sleeve to pull her away before she was struck by Monica's hockey stick.

"You nosy witches!" Monica yelled before throwing back her arm, ready to take another swipe with her stick.

"Move!" Lilly snapped, shoving Abigail. The two of them bolted between their vehicles as Monica made another swing. Thankfully she missed them both but the momentum continued and she struck the passenger side window of Abigail's car with such force it shattered.

"My car!"

"Forget your car, Abigail, just run!"

Monica continued to swing and yell at them as they charged across the car park. Running blindly with no idea where they were headed, they dashed down an alleyway between two buildings. A dire mistake. It was a dead end, and they had nowhere left to run. They turned back to the entrance just as Monica appeared, panting slightly but still brandishing her hockey stick.

"She's going to kill us with that stupid stick," Abigail sobbed, clutching Lilly's arm.

"You two," Monica hissed. "Are going to ruin everything."

"Monica, let me help you," Lilly said gently. "I know you wrote that letter to Carol Ann. It was to try to drive a wedge between her and Joseph, wasn't it? So she'd believe he thought her a burden and an embarrassment?"

Monica nodded once but stayed silent, continuing to stare with utter hatred at Lilly.

"That bit at the end, about him not wanting to do something he would regret? It was supposed to make her think he would have her sectioned, put in a mental institution wasn't it?"

"Lilly, what are you doing?" Abigail hissed. "Shut up or you'll make her even crazier."

But Lilly knew she needed to try to calm the girl down. Keep her talking so they could either disarm her or get away. She shrugged Abigail off and took a step forward.

"She realised it was you who'd written it though, didn't she?" This was a complete guess on Lilly's part, but an educated one.

Monica gritted her teeth. "Yes. She recognised my writing from the reunion invitations. It was a stupid mistake. Next thing I know, she's here looking for me. Wanting to talk to me about it. About me stealing her husband. Said she was worried about me. Can you believe it? The local crazy woman worried about me!"

"So you drugged her?"

Monica shrugged. "It wasn't difficult. I just added a little something to her tea while we talked in the garden. It relaxed her. I suggested a walk. It was easy to get her down to the river after that."

"Then you forced her to take an overdose of the medications you stole from the lab."

Monica scowled. "Well, aren't you the clever one? It was easy, she was so high she practically drowned herself. But you won't be telling anyone else." She stepped closer, brandishing the stick, a look of crazed menace in her eyes.

Lilly felt Abigail once again grab her arm. "Stand your ground," Lilly muttered. "And we can try to get that hockey stick away from her..." Abigail whimpered as Monica came nearer, getting ready to swing.

Chapter Thirteen

*L*ILLY FELT LIKE a caged animal as Monica came nearer. "We go at her at the same time," she whispered to Abigail, who looked far from keen on the idea. Unfortunately, Monica wasn't giving them any other option. It was clear she was determined to keep her secrets, even if meant beating two women to death with a hockey stick. Though how she thought she was going to get away with it, Lilly had no idea. She'd obviously been pushed to breaking point and was no longer rational.

Lilly moved forward and let out a brief sigh of relief when Abigail followed her lead. Monica swung directly at them but was momentarily taken off guard when both Lilly and Abigail lunged forward. The hockey stick connected with Abigail's shoulder, but Lilly had already grabbed Monica's arm, which slowed down the swing and lessened the impact.

"Ow!" Abigail yelled, grabbing the stick and wrenching it from the girl's hands. She threw it to the ground.

"That's enough, Monica," Lilly said in a firm tone, still holding her arm. She was about to try to calm things down when Abigail decided she'd had enough.

Furious at the damage to her car, having to run in fear across a car park and being cornered like an animal and threatened, she lashed out, violently pushing Monica who slipped and fell to the ground. She was on the verge of kicking her when Lilly pushed her aside. "Stop it! You can't go around kicking people, Abigail! And she's pregnant, remember."

Stopping to squabble was a big mistake because as soon as they were distracted Monica rolled over, snatched up her hockey stick and stood up. "Look out!" Abigail yelled just in time for Lilly to avoid being smacked on the back of the head.

However, their positions had reversed, and they now found themselves with a free run out of the alley. They turned and bolted back the way they'd come.

"Where is everybody?" Lilly wheezed as they dashed across the deserted car park.

"Let's just get back to the car and call the police," Abigail gasped.

Lilly quickly glanced behind them and saw Monica on their tail. But she must have damaged her ankle when she fell, as she was limping. By some unspoken agreement, they made their way to Lilly's undamaged car first, only to find she'd not got her keys.

"I must have dropped them back there."

"You can't go back for them. Quick, we'll have to take mine. Get in."

Lilly grabbed the handle and yanked open the passenger door, only to see the glass from the window on the seat. She slammed the door, opened the rear one and launched herself across the back seat. "Quick, go!" she yelled, just as Monica reached them.

Abigail threw the car into drive and peeled out of the parking space to the sound of squealing tyres and the smell of burning rubber. Lilly, who hadn't had time to put on her seatbelt, went crashing to the foot well, bashing her elbow as she did so.

"She's following us," Abigail cried as she accelerated, causing Lilly, who'd just crawled onto the seat to fall sideways and bang her head on the door.

"Abigail, will you calm down! Let me get my seatbelt on."

Abigail slowed down a fraction, enabling Lilly to get strapped in.

"Lilly?"

"What?"

"You don't suppose Monica has a car, do you?"

*L*ILLY FUMBLED IN her pocket for her phone, her intention to call the police.

"Abigail, drive to the police station, I'm calling them now." She switched on her phone. "Oh, no. I must have pocket dialled Stacey by mistake."

"Never mind Stacey, whoever she is," yelled Abigail. "Call the police, she's right behind us! Good grief, I can hardly see a thing out of this windscreen."

Lilly turned to look out of the rear window, and sure enough there was a small black car speeding in their direction. "Put your foot down," she shouted, now wishing they had remained at the university and tried to get to a classroom rather than turning this into a high-speed car chase. The likes of which had never been seen in Plumpton Mallet in all the years she'd lived there.

Abigail accelerated, speeding down the road towards the outskirts of town when a red traffic light caught them. She tapped the brake. "Are you mad? Don't stop" Lilly shouted from the backseat. "She's gaining on us."

"Right... right." Abigail stammered, speeding through the light.

Lilly turned back just in time to see Monica following them through the red light and another vehicle slamming into her from the oncoming intersection. "Stop!" Lilly yelled, recognising the other car. "That's Stacey."

Abigail slowed down and pulled over to the side of the road. Lilly tossed her phone at her. "Get the police and an ambulance here, now," she said. Abigail fiddled with the phone, her hands shaking so much she could barely hold it, but Lilly didn't notice, she was already out of the car and running back up the road towards the accident.

Monica's car had been flipped upside down. Stacey, on the other hand, seemed relatively unscathed as she exited her vehicle. The front end was bashed in as a result of the impact, but considering the force with which she'd hit, the damage was remarkably little.

"I can't believe you just walked away from that impact. Are you all right?" Lilly asked, noting the nosebleed and the cut above her eyebrow.

"I'm good. My car's too old for airbags, apparently, but the seatbelts are just fine."

"What are you doing here?" Lilly demanded. It came out sharper than she'd meant.

"Are you kidding?" Stacey said. "You called me. I could hear you and knew you were in trouble, so I closed the shop and headed out after I called the police."

Lilly pulled the girl in for a quick hug. "You're amazing. Thank you." She said. Then turned to Monica's car.

They hurried over, kneeling on the road by the driver's side window. Monica groaned.

"Monica, stay still an ambulance is on the way."

Lilly knew better than to try to move her. There was no smoke and no smell of petrol, so the car wasn't in imminent danger of catching fire. She held the girl's hand and talked to her gently.

"My leg..." Monica gasped.

"Try not to move, you'll be out of here very soon. I promise."

Cars were braking all around them, completely blocking the crossroads as people stopped, exiting their vehicles in an effort to either see what had happened or to help. Several were on phones reporting the accident to the police, but thanks to Stacey's earlier call they were already on their way and a couple of police cars and a two ambulances arrived a few minutes later.

"My baby." Monica cried, her free hand resting on her stomach. She turned to look at Lilly, the crazed look she'd had before had completely vanished, replaced with fear. She looked like a terrified child, and Lilly couldn't help her heart twist in sympathy.

"Try not to worry, Monica. The ambulance is here. They'll take good care of you both."

Monica took a last look at Lilly before breaking down in tears. "I'm sorry. I'm so sorry."

ONCE THE POLICE were busy calming the chaos and trying to clear the scene of onlookers and their obstructing vehicles, Abigail got out of her car and walked over to the crash. She'd managed to find a notebook and pen and was about to speak to Monica, who had been extracted from her vehicle and loaded onto a stretcher, when a fierce look from Lilly made her think otherwise. She slipped her notebook in her pocket with a contrite look. But as usual, she had to get the last word.

The ambulance was about to set off with Monica in the back, when Abigail informed a police man that the girl had attacked them with a hockey stick and caused massive damage to her car. A confirming nod from Lilly and he elected to travel to the hospital with Monica.

A paramedic from the second ambulance was busy talking to Stacey.

"You need to get to hospital too," he said, shining a light in her eyes. "You've got a mild concussion."

"No, sorry. I can't afford it."

"Stacey," Lilly said. "It doesn't cost you here like it does in America. You need to get yourself checked out, okay?"

"Oh, right? I forgot. Yeah, okay, I'll go. I am a bit dizzy."

"I'll come and see you shortly."

Stacey handed over her car keys to the waiting police officer and moments later was in the second ambulance on her way to hospital. Lilly surveyed the scene with a combination of horror and sorrow.

"Dreadful isn't it." Abigail said, coming up behind her.

Lilly nodded in agreement.

"I mean, how on earth am I to do without my car? The insurance process takes so long, and no doubt I'll be given some inferior model to use in the interim. It's already cost me a small fortune in repairs recently."

Lilly stared at her, aghast. Luckily, she was saved from speaking her mind as Bonnie drew up in a police car and came over.

"Lilly, I heard on my radio about the accident and came as quick as I could. Are you both all right?"

"Yes, we're fine. Just a few bumps and bruises, mainly."

"Speak for yourself," Abigail retorted. "My car is a complete mess. Not to mention I was nearly bludgeoned to death by a hockey stick wielding maniac."

Bonnie raised an eyebrow. Lilly quickly shook her head.

"Right. Well, we'll need to take full statements from you both. Abigail, if you'll go to my colleague over there, please. Lilly, I'll take yours."

"Can you give me a lift back to St John's?" Lilly asked Bonnie once Abigail had gone. "My car is still there, and I lost my keys in the car park."

"Yes, all right, we can talk on the way."

Bonnie executed a perfect three-point turn, then let out an exasperated sigh. "So, which part of *don't get involved* and *leave it to the professionals* didn't you understand, Lilly Tweed?" She demanded as they journeyed back to the university.

"Ah, you're angry with me?"

"Of course I'm angry with you, you could have been killed. What on earth did you think you were doing?"

Lilly laid her head back, closed her eyes, and related the entire story from start to finish. Bonnie had reached their destination long before Lilly had completed her story, so parked up and listened in silence. Eventually, Lilly opened her eyes and sat up. "So, that's what happened."

"God, Lilly. Don't ever do anything like this again. You've been very lucky. So, you're saying Monica Morris confessed to killing Carol Ann Hotch."

"Yes."

"And she was responsible for the laboratory thefts, too?"

"Yes, I think so. She didn't deny it when I asked her, anyway. The stolen drugs are the same as those Carol Ann was forced to overdose on."

"I'll need to radio all this in and make sure she has a twenty-four guard at the hospital at the very least. You go and find your keys and I'll come and help in a minute."

"Don't worry, you go and do your job, Bonnie. I can get a taxi if I have to."

"Okay, if you're sure?" Bonnie paused. "Look, I'm not condoning what you did, Lilly, but it looks like you've solved a couple of cases for us. So, thank you."

"Does this mean I'm forgiven?"

Bonnie smirked. "Of course. Just stay out of trouble."

It didn't take Lilly long to find her keys, they were in the alley where the main scuffle had taken place. She scooped them up and walked wearily back to her car. She was just unlocking the door when her phone rang. It was Archie.

"LILLY, WHAT'S THIS I hear about yet another car crash? Abigail's just called, claiming she's got the scoop of the century."

Lilly laughed. "A bit of an exaggeration, but yes, it's a big story as far as Plumpton Mallet is concerned. Actually, come to think of it, it's a pretty big story anywhere, so may even end up in the nationals."

"You've got to give me the scoop first, Lilly," Archie said, but Lilly hesitated.

"You've really put me on the spot here, you know, Archie. I don't want to be in the middle of you two. I told Abigail what I knew because she was here and had almost worked it out for herself anyway. I made her promise that she would tell you everything first though so you could put the article together between you."

"The only reason she was there at all, was because she swiped all my notes!" Archie cried down the phone. "She thinks I don't know, but I've been putting all this together from the start and the only way she'd make those connections is through my hard work. I tell you, I'm just about at the end of my tether with that woman."

Lilly gasped. "She stole your notes? Oh, Archie, I'm sorry I had no idea. That really is beyond the pale. Is that how she found out about Monica?"

"How did you find out about Monica?"

"Hang on, let me get in my car and I'll tell you everything."

For the second time in an hour Lilly went through the entire sequence of events, stopping occasionally while Archie asked questions and confirmed sources. At the end, Archie let out an appreciative whistle.

"Wow, Abigail was right, that's some story."

Lilly wasn't exactly a fan of Abigail, she'd taken Lilly's job at the paper and gone out of her way to make her life difficult because of the agony aunt letter box outside her shop. Now it turned out she'd also pinched Archie's notes. But on the other hand, Abigail had broken down and told Lilly how desperate she was. That must have taken some courage for a woman like her. She couldn't afford to lose her job and in no way did Lilly want to be even partly responsible for that if it happened.

"Archie, I've told you everything and you now know exactly what Abigail does. You're on a level playing field. But please, will you try to work it out with her? She's worried sick she's going to lose her job, and she has nothing else to fall back on."

"And so she should be," said Archie tetchily. "Her agony aunt column is a disaster, and the investigative pieces she did on the university break-ins were very poorly constructed."

"That may be so, Archie. Not everyone can write as well as you. But you have to admit she was right about the drug dealing side of the thefts. Why not take this opportunity to let her learn from a master, Archie? She actually has quite good instincts when she puts her mind to it. And she enjoys running around and following up leads. She could be an asset to you if you let her."

Archie sighed dramatically. "Oh, all right. Here's what I'll do. I'm going to talk to Abigail, and I'll suggest we co-write the main article together. I'll also inform her that I know she took my notes. So she'll have to say yes to my very magnanimous offer. However, after that I want an exclusive interview with you about your role in solving the case, okay? Just you and me over a cup of your delicious tea."

Lilly laughed. "Yes, okay, I'll happily do that for you. Although, a glass of wine in the local pub would be a welcome change to tea."

"Done!" Archie said. "I might even treat you to dinner."

"Now that sounds like a proper plan. Listen, I've got to get to the hospital and see how Stacey is. She got quite banged up saving our bacon. I'll call you when I leave and we can discuss where to go for that dinner."

"All right. I hope Stacey's okay. See you later, Lilly," he said, and hung up the phone.

*I*T TOOK LILLY half an hour to get to the hospital. Then another ten minutes to find a parking space, find the right change for the meter, get a ticket to put on her dashboard and walk back to the A&E department. At the desk she was told to wait and someone would come and get her when Stacey was able to receive visitors. She was assured, however, that the girl wasn't severely injured. The doctor's were purely keeping her under observation for the time being.

She wandered over to the seating area just as Joseph Hotch rushed up to the counter in a frantic, dishevelled state. She turned and hurried back.

"Joseph, what are you doing here? Are you all right?"

"Lilly, do you know what's happened? I got a call saying there'd been an accident?"

"Yes, I was there, I'm afraid. Who called you?"

"Someone from here. The ward sister, I think. She, Monica that is, gave my name," he paused, looking sick and wretched. "Lilly, is Monica pregnant? Do you know?"

She studied him for a moment and saw the guilt along with the pain. There was no denying he knew her now. He must have realised how pointless it was. "Yes, she is."

"And she did it, didn't she? She killed my wife?"

"Yes. She confessed to Abigail and me earlier. I'm so sorry, Joseph."

He staggered to the nearest chair and collapsed into it, head in hands. Lilly followed and sat beside him.

"It's all my fault," he sobbed.

"No, it's not. You can't blame yourself for what Monica did, Joseph. She's an adult and accountable for her own actions."

"I would have taken responsibility for the child and looked after them both, if only she'd told me. She didn't have to hurt Carol Ann. Oh my god, what have I done?"

Lilly sat with him while he poured his heart out. Telling her about the difficult life he'd had with Carol Ann as her mental health deteriorated. The flattery he'd felt when a young woman had shown an interest in him. *He wasn't the first man who'd had his head turned by a pretty girl*, Lilly thought. *Nor would he be the last.* But this affair had ended in the ultimate tragedy and ruined many lives. The ripples of which would be felt for a long time. It would take Joseph Hotch years to put the pieces of his life back together.

Lilly sat with the distraught man for over an hour. Eventually the crying ceased, and he began to pull himself together.

"What are you going to do, Joseph?" she asked gently.

"I don't know," he said, wiping his eyes. "I have no idea what to do. I can't think straight." He looked up at her, "I don't suppose you have any advice, do you?"

Lilly thought for a moment, then nodded as an idea took hold. "I think I might have some if you're willing to listen."

Chapter Fourteen

FIVE MINUTES AFTER she'd opened the shop the next morning, Lilly was surprised to Stacey walk in. She'd told her at the hospital, when she'd eventually been allowed to visit, not to bother coming in, to rest until she felt better.

"Stacey, what are you doing here? Are you all right?"

"I feel fine, don't worry."

"Well, you don't look it," Lilly said, peering at the two black eyes Stacey now sported.

Stacey waved her off. "It looks worse than it is."

Oh, to be young again, Lilly thought. She'd had a restless night with her swollen elbow and the bruise on her temple where she'd been thrown around in the back of Abigail's car.

"Well, you must promise me you'll go home if you start to feel poorly."

"I will. I've got pain medication from the hospital so I should be okay."

At nine o'clock Lilly turned the shop sign to open, and the day began in earnest. Customers were still coming in to discuss the theft, and Stacey brewed tea samples and tisanes and deftly sold them merchandise before they left. At ten o'clock a car Lilly didn't recognise pulled up outside and Abigail Douglas got out. She rushed to the agony aunt letter box, stuffed something inside, then returned to the car. Driving away without even a glance through the window.

How curious, Lilly thought as she went to retrieve what Abigail had posted. It was the morning edition of The Plumpton Mallet Gazette. She unfolded it and emblazoned across the cover was a candid shot of herself at the site of the accident speaking with a police officer. She hadn't even realised someone had taken it. The headline read; **Local Teashop Owner Turns Super-sleuth.** Lilly's cheeks burned as she turned to page three where the story continued. The by-line read *Archie Brown* and just below that *with Abigail Douglas*. At the bottom scrawled in red pen was a note. *Thanks, Lilly. AD.*

"Well, I'll be," she said out loud, smiling. Archie had told her he'd informed Abigail the only reason he was agreeing to a co-written article and not having her demoted or sacked for stealing his notes, was because Lilly had vouched for her. Thanks were completely out of character for Abigail. Perhaps there was still a chance the two of them could get along after all.

She closed the paper, she'd read it properly later, and turned back to the shop, surprised to find it was almost full.

She'd been so engrossed in the article she'd shut out her surroundings completely.

"Sorry, Stacey," she said when she got back behind the counter. "I didn't realise we'd got so busy."

It turned out the place was packed because everyone who'd read the paper that morning had decided to turn up at the shop and congratulate its proprietor and her lovely American sales assistant. Several of them had papers tucked under their arms and were insistent on reading out sections and peppering her with questions as to how she'd managed to solve the case. Stacey insisted on getting photographs of everything for social media, encouraging patrons to do the same if they had accounts. "It will put this place on the map!" she told Lilly with a grin. She was quite happy to have her photo taken with two black eyes, so how could Lilly refuse when all she had was a bruised temple and cheekbone in a fetching shade of violet?

Eventually there was a brief lull and while Stacey retired to the back room for lunch, Lilly took the opportunity to read the article in full. It was clear Archie had done his research. The story was well written and full of detailed information, most of which she had provided over an excellent dinner and a bottle of wine the previous evening. He must have worked through the night to get the article written in time for the morning edition.

Abigail had interviewed Stacey over the phone while she was at the hospital, so had included a couple of quotes from her. Archie, as well as formally interviewing Lilly, had even managed to speak briefly with Joseph Hotch.

The first half of the article was mainly concerned with how Lilly had pieced together clues and eventually realised who the murderer of Carol Ann Hotch was. For her part Lilly had told Archie most of it was dumb luck, but he'd waved away that idea. It mentioned Bonnie as being an integral part of the investigation, complimenting the local police and their efforts, despite the original incorrect assumption that Barney Darwin had been the guilty party due to his attempted theft of the victim's pocket watch.

With no proof that he hadn't bought the watch from Carol Ann, and with the watch safely back with Joseph, he had been released with a hefty fine and a warning. His reputation in tatters.

But it was the second half of the article which interested Lilly the most. Apart from a broken leg, Monica had come out of the accident in one piece. But more importantly, her baby was unharmed. Joseph had taken Lilly's advice and had spent a long time talking through the future with Monica, and they had agreed he would be raising his child alone. Monica would be serving a long prison sentence, and it was likely the baby would be an adult if and when she was ever released. She had therefore willingly signed over all parental rights to the father. While it wasn't in the paper, Joseph had shared with Lilly the fact that if it was a girl, he would name her after his wife.

She knew Joseph had a lot to work through; the consequences of his decisions and actions had had a catastrophic outcome, so she'd taken the liberty of handing over Dr Jorgensen's details to him. Whether he sought out the doctor was up to him, but Lilly felt sure he would.

She sighed, wondering what would become of them all. Then folding the newspaper put it under the counter. It was time to turn her attention back to her proper business. Several customers had entered.

Lilly knew everyone who ventured in over the next half hour, apart from one older gentleman who had positioned himself in a corner and hadn't moved the entire time she was busy serving. Eventually it was just the browsers who were left, so she approached him with a smile.

"Hello. Can I help you with anything?"

He glanced round the shop. "I was looking for someone. But perhaps she's not here today?"

"Who is it you're looking for?"

"Stacey Pepper. I do have the right shop, don't I?"

"Yes, she's at lunch at the moment, though. Sorry, who are you?"

The man gave Lilly a fixed look. "My name is James. James Pepper. And I need to speak with my daughter."

If you enjoyed *Tea & Sympathy*, the first book in the series of the same name, please leave a review on Amazon. It really does help and you'd make the author very happy.

About the Author

J. New is the author of *THE YELLOW COTTAGE VINTAGE MYSTERIES,* traditional English whodunits with a twist, set in the 1930's. Known for their clever humour as well as the interesting slant on the traditional murder mystery, they have all achieved Bestseller status on Amazon.

J. New also writes two contemporary cozy crime series:

THE TEA & SYMPATHY series featuring Lilly Tweed, former newspaper Agony Aunt now purveyor of fine teas at The Tea Emporium in the small English market town of Plumpton Mallet. Along with a regular cast of characters, including Earl Grey the shop cat.

THE FINCH & FISCHER series featuring mobile librarian Penny Finch and her rescue dog Fischer. Follow them as they dig up clues and sniff out red herrings in the six villages and hamlets that make up Hampsworthy Downs.

Jacquie was born in West Yorkshire, England. She studied art and design and after qualifying began work as an interior designer, moving onto fine art restoration and animal portraiture before making the decision to pursue her lifelong ambition to write. She now writes full time and lives with her partner of twenty-two years, two dogs and five cats, all of whom she rescued.

If you would like to be kept up to date with new releases from J. New, you can sign up to her *Reader's Group* on her website www.jnewwrites.com You will also receive a link to download the free e-book, *The Yellow Cottage Mystery*, the short-story prequel to The Yellow Cottage Vintage Mystery series.

Made in United States
North Haven, CT
14 December 2024

62542595R00109